A WIZARD AND HER DAUGHTER

MATTHEW RUNYON

Orchards and Lessons

Hannah called back over her shoulder through the doorway. "We should be home by midday, Cirie, if the trees aren't too stubborn."

Ciaran's deep voice rumbled back, amused, "Then I'll expect you near sundown, shall I? Good thing one of you had sense enough to remember the food. I can rely on *her*, at least."

Leyla giggled, rushing out the door with a sturdy wicker basket in one hand and her stout walking stick in the other. "Right, Papa! I'll make sure Mama eats, and drinks, and takes a rest, and doesn't get distracted trying to learn the names of *all* the trees, and—"

Her mother gave an exaggerated, long-suffering sigh. "Yes, yes, I'm forgetful and distractible and would *surely* starve without my family nudging me to take a bite now and then. But I'll want you to remember all this the next time we're all warm and snug at midwinter, and see if you think learning the house's name was a waste of time then!"

A deep chuckle joined the next round of giggles, and Hannah's wide grin kept those giggles going for a fair step along the path that eventually led to the orchard. It was a lovely summer day, and watching the sun slowly roll up over the hills and shimmer on the river kept Leyla quiet for a good long while. Hannah was impressed when it was a whole six, maybe seven minutes before the first questions came.

"Mama, how much of the trees' names *are* we going to learn today? Are we actually going to learn *each* tree's name? I know I told Papa I wouldn't let you, but it could be our secret!"

Hannah had to fight to keep her smile from being too big. Laughing *with* Leyla was one thing, but her daughter wasn't quick to forgive being laughed *at*. "I wondered when the questions would start, Ley-ley! No, we aren't going to learn each tree's name; that would be a little too much for what your Uncle Lachlan wants us to do. Trees are growing things, and their names change all the time. Little by little, of course, but unless we wanted to come back every week, it wouldn't make the spell any better, and it might make it worse. The name of the orchard should be enough. The earth they eat, the water they drink, the sun they bask in…that will work for what we need."

She kept answering Leyla's questions as they strode along, remembering back to her own apprenticeship, and how everything had seemed new and wonderful when she could finally accompany her aunt Aoife on the rounds. It was all *different* when you were there, instead of just hearing about it at home. She smiled as she looked down at her daughter, and hoped Aoife would be proud to see her lessons passed down to her grand-niece. Eventually she started quizzing her daughter on the usual types of protections for orchards, and between that and enjoying the gorse scattered like coins of gold among the fresh, resinous pine forest, they filled the hour's walk easily.

When they turned down the orchard lane, Leyla looked up eagerly, and Hannah nodded grinning approval before ostentatiously covering her ears. Leyla scrambled through the basket for a few moments before finding a small piece of wool cloth with a circle of graceful curves and flourishes worked into it. She pressed it up against her throat, breathed deeply, and then shouted *far* more loudly than even the most excitable child could manage, *"Uncle Lachlan, we're here!"*

Hannah swept her eyes up and down Leyla, watching surreptitiously for any signs of exhaustion, and resisted the urge to put her hand to her daughter's head to check for fever. She'd looked over the spell already; she knew it wouldn't take too much energy (and might actually just take barely enough that Leyla would *sit still* for their work today), she *knew* it was safe... But it was still the first spell her little girl had designed herself, and every nightmare of something like what happened to poor Matthew Half-a-hand ran through her head in a jumble. They both had been just about Leyla's age...

But Leyla just staggered a bit before carefully lowering her *successful* spell back into the basket and whooping and celebrating. "I did it! I did it, I did it, I did it, I *did* it! Mama, did you hear? I bet Papa heard it all the way back home, I was *so loud*!" Her walking stick and the basket were flailing about wildly as she did a little victory dance.

Hannah's smile was so wide it hurt, and she (mostly) dodged the stick and basket to wrap Leyla up in a big hug, spinning her around in the air. "I'm so proud of you! Now you're a *real* apprentice!" And if while she was spinning Leyla and holding her close, she was quietly checking for any fever or tremors, then what her daughter didn't know wouldn't hurt any feelings. Though, admittedly, how Hannah would tell tremors from the vibrating of an excited ten-year-old was a bit of a pickle…

A boisterous shout reached them. "Oho! And here I thought I was just getting *one* wizard to work on my little orchard!" Lachlan's beefy form followed, and he grinned at the sight of Hannah and Leyla. Hannah would have sworn this was impossible, but Leyla squiggled even more at being called a wizard for the first time. She escaped her mother and, handing her stick and basket off, ran down the lane and jumped at her uncle. He caught her up in a bear hug, unfazed by the impact, and the spinning resumed with a new adult as the fulcrum. Hannah followed more sedately, juggling two walking sticks, the basket, and her equipment pack.

"Now, 'Lan, how am I supposed to get that ward built if you've absconded with my partner here?" Hannah's mock-severe question was followed by a quick kiss on his cheek, which she had to time carefully to avoid getting a walking stick tangled in her daughter's twirling legs.

"Ach, well, wouldn't want to deprive you now, would I?" He gave his niece one last squeeze before setting her back on the packed earth, and enfolding Hannah in turn. "Not that you've been deprived—I can see Ciaran's taking good care of you, more meat on your bones now. You can tell my brother that I've *nearly* forgiven him for stealing you away."

Hannah chuckled, shaking her head. "Lachlan Martin, it's been over a dozen years, and you've said that every time you see me. I must have been a twig back then, if Cirie's been putting 'more meat on my bones' for all that time."

Leyla grinned up at them, enjoying the familiar interplay.

Lachlan nodded gravely. "Aye, that you were, and still the brightest one at the Fair, perhaps the whole of the Free Rivers. How you managed that, when you must have been *starving* all the time, I'll never know." He chuckled and held his hands up in surrender after Hannah tapped his head tartly with one of the walking sticks. "All right, all right, mayhaps you aren't all *that* much meatier now, but you look happier each time all the same. He must be doing *something* right, and that's enough for me. And Calvin agrees, so it has to be true."

Hannah gave the basket and stick back to Leyla, and they all began moving up the lane, breathing deeply of the subtle scent of the cherry trees. "And that's another thing, 'Lan: You can't tell me you're still broken up about me when you went off and got married a whole *month* later. And Calvin hasn't bashed your head in with a frying pan yet, so things must still be going along at least middling well."

"It was the heartbreak that drove me into his arms! And unless you've changed your mind, there's none other for me, and things are tolerable enough, yes…"

"*Lachlan Martin*, do you expect me to believe for one moment that—"

"Mama, look! There's the waterwheel! Ooh, it's so big, we're going to be able to do a really good ward, aren't we?"

Hannah came out of the well-worn rut of her friendly bicker with her brother-by-marriage to give an approving nod. "That we are, Ley-ley, that we are. Good work there, *brother* mine. I know it took a pretty penny to get the metal work on that, but it won't take long to pay for itself."

Lachlan gave a deeply satisfied nod. "Aye, the better yields'll do that quick enough, and it'll be that much more secure for little Annabelle when she inherits. Don't know how much more a man can do than hand his girl a warded orchard, a good home, and a good education. It all costs, aye, but she'll be able to make a case for being a bonnet laird, eventually, and that would be quite a thing."

Hannah nodded agreeably. She wasn't so sure the title was worth trying to fight for, but her niece was going to be all ready to run the land better even than her parents, and that was saying more than a little. And looking over the wheel, she realised that Lachlan had not oversold her on how much power there would be. He'd made good use of the rapids that made the river unnavigable to elevate the water entering the wheel, and that would add substantially to the efficiency.

"Now, Leyla, what's the first step we need to do to figure out our warding spell?"

"Find out how much power we can use! Uncle Lachlan, how many light spells can your waterwheel power?"

"Well, I believe they said about—"

"Apprentice Leyla, are you going to trust what *someone else* tells you about power?"

Leyla's face fell at the sharp tone from her mother. "N-no, Wizard Hannah, that's right, we should test it ourselves and see. 'A good wizard never trusts when she can verify.'"

Hannah nodded firmly, took off her pack, found the stencil and chalk, and handed them to her daughter. "Go verify, Apprentice, and then we can plan."

Leyla nodded and went off inside the housing of the wheel structure to the rotating axle. She checked the spell inscribed there, saw it was the usual one, and started using the stencil and chalk to trace copy after copy of the intricate and flowing spellscript onto the large stone adjacent to the axle. Each one, when completed, began to glow softly in the dimness, until the thirty-first spell remained just chalk. Leyla counted the spells, then counted them again, just like her mother had taught her, before nodding and running back outside.

"Thirty, Wizard Hannah! Thirty lightsworth of power!"

Hannah raised her eyebrows. She had guessed they would have twenty-five to work with, and this would change her plan. "Let me come see, Apprentice… Hm, yes, thirty it is. That engineer really was worth all the hassle. Wonder if we could use the same technique to— Bah, not now, Hannah. Do the work and *then* think about experiments." She shook her head slowly and wandered back out of the wheel housing, lost in thought.

"Lachlan, with that much power… If we can figure out a good enough name for the orchard…I know I said we would only be able to do a few pest wards and a general strength ward, but I *think* we could fit wind and frost wards in, too."

"Well, I'd not be one to say I told you so, Hannah, but, ah—"

"Yes, yes, you were right, I underestimated the magnificence of your wheel. Now I just have to make sure you don't regret hiring us instead of one of the Guild wizards." The words were said lightly, but Lachlan could see Hannah's fingers drumming faster. He wisely forbore to comment as the rangy wizard continued.

"Hm…the wind and frost wards won't work at the same time. If we get a sleet storm like we did the year Leyla was born, you'll still have to use the backup frost ward, but… yes, I think we can do it. Ley-ley, we are going to have to learn a very good name for this orchard. I think your father was right after all." She had a soft smile. "He usually is, about me… So, let's start with the sunlight, then the water, then the soil, and see where we are then. I have my stencil on the type of tree already, copied it when your uncle bought the seedlings, so that's done, at least."

Hannah began pulling out her supplies.

"Now, Apprentice, why are we starting with the sunlight part of the orchard's name?"

Leyla screwed up her face in thought while her fingers sought for the right stencils in the pack.

"Because…It changes the most?"

Hannah nodded approvingly as she set the standard sunlight stencil for the village environs down on her test cloth and began tracing the patterns in chalk. "Aye, and so we'll need to test it a few different times throughout the day. Noon-day sun won't change much, but the shape of the hills and mountains can change things near the beginning and end of the day, and that changes how the trees grow, and so their name."

Leyla nodded back, tracing another variant of the standard light spell as they sat in the shade together. "I can see that…Then the water changes, but not as much as the sunlight, and the soil changes even less, and the trees least of all, and we already have a good name for the trees anyway, so that's why the order matters."

"Right, Ley-ley. Now, you've checked your spell? Good, let's switch then." They leaned over, careful to avoid disturbing their respective work, and thoroughly checked the other's spell, before trading nods. Leyla then gathered a small piece of carefully marked wood, and placed it where the light spell expected to draw its power from. Hannah first closed the linkage between the name and the light spell, and then with only a few motherly twinges allowed Leyla to close the final activation line on the light spell.

Her daughter drew a straight line across the final gap from the stencil, set as usual opposite where the wood was placed to make it less likely for someone to accidentally power the spell with their own energy, and simultaneously the spell lit up and the wood flared. This spell was set to only last for a short, but precise, time to help with measurements like this. Once it ceased lighting, and the wood ceased flaring, Leyla counted out how many marked increments on the wood remained. "Only three left, Wizard Hannah."

Hannah's brows furrowed. She'd been hoping for five… But, this was why Lachlan had hired her, after all. A better name would get them better enough efficiencies. "Well, Apprentice, we have our work cut out for us then. Let's see about changing this section of the sunlight name here, I think it's getting more light than it expects, we're a little higher here than the village proper…"

The rest of the day was spent in the same pattern: Testing, experimenting with changes to the names, and more testing to measure the impacts. Meticulous work, and taking plenty of concentration, but Hannah was pleased to see she and her daughter worked well together. She had thought they would, but it had been hard not to worry after years spent with only her own company in her craft.

Often, Hannah would talk to Leyla as she experimented. "This is the section about the temperature of the water, you see how similar it is to this part about how strong the sunlight is? Both of them are measuring how hot or cold they are. My standard water one was made near town, it's a little warmer there because it's farther from the mountains, let's try changing this…"

Sometimes, Leyla would ask questions or suggest something. "Mama, I was thinking, maybe the soil near the river has different critters and things living in it than the soil farther away? Should we do a couple of names, instead of just one?"

And every so often, they would have a breakthrough: "Aha, that's it! It's the irrigation channels that are throwing us off. My standard name is for just a ditch, but your uncle lined his in clay! I took the clay into account on the soil, but not on the water…"

But, eventually, they had it. They checked their calculations, ran them again, did one final experiment using a wind spell and counteracting ward, then a frost spell and counteracting ward, but they had it. It wasn't one name, in the end, but it wasn't a name for each tree either.

Hannah stretched, stiff from a day spent bending and examining and sketching, and she and Leyla went down one of the rows to where Lachlan was uprooting a small patch of weeds. "I think we have it, Lachlan. Ciaran should be able to turn these into a proper spell stencil, and we've got enough to handle all the wards."

"That's right amazing, Hannah, and glad I am to hear it! Always worth it to pay for a real expert! And, ah, if I might ask, what kind of margin do we have?"

Hannah smirked, hand on her hip. "Lachlan, what kind of wizard do you take me for? You know I don't present work unless I've got a margin of at *least* ten percent on it."

Lachlan whistled. "Hannah my love, that's right wizardry, that is. I wouldn't have thought—"

"Weellll...I *will* have to see if Cirie can make them small enough. We had to do five different names, in the end, with the changes in water flow and a *surprisingly* large difference between what lives in the soil around the trees next to the river and next to the various ditches. Fitting all that onto the power stone is going to be a bit tricky, but I think he can manage it."

Lachlan nodded slowly. "Well, I'll be a monkey's uncle."

"Hey!" Leyla said. "I'm not a monkey! I'm a wizard 'prentice!"

The big man laughed and snagged her into a bear hug. "That you are, that you are indeed! And now you two need to get home—you know how your father gets if you're late."

"Oooh, he's right Mama, we need to hurry!"

Hannah looked at the sky and winced, giving Lachlan a quick squeeze and then setting off down the lane. "I...think we can make it home in time, if we don't dawdle, but you're right, come on Ley-ley."

Lachlan waved them off, and went back to weeding as the two strode away.

They made it back home before sundown...barely. But it was a cheery, welcoming sight, with the firelight showing from the window and the twilit breeze twining the wonderful scent of the sweet peas around them. But best of all, at least to his wife, was Ciaran coming to the door as he heard them approaching. "There you are! I was *almost* about to get worried. How was your day?"

He took their sticks, the now-empty basket, and the equipment pack, setting them in their proper places, and then wrapped both of them up in his arms.

"Oh, Papa, it was wonderful! My spell worked! We figured out five names for the orchard, and Mama thinks we can do a really good ward, and Uncle Lachlan was so impressed and he called me a wizard and oooooh, that smells good Papa…"

Ciaran chuckled, giving his wife a tolerably amused look while she looked slightly chagrined. "*Five* names, hm? I suppose I'll have my work cut out for me for the next few weeks. Now, take your boots off, wash your hands and faces, and we can have a proper dinner together. And, both of you—"

The tone of his deep voice matched the loving smile on his face.

"Welcome home."

Sheepdog

Hannah yawned and stretched as she made her way blearily out the door. "And this is why your father made up our basket last night. He's no one's fool, and doesn't wake up at this hour if he can help it."

Leyla outdid her mother's yawn with an open-mouthed sound more reminiscent of an annoyed cat than anything else, which she ended with an unhappy mrowl. "I think Papa has the right idea. It's not even dawn yet! Do we *have* to go now?"

A not-very-suppressed sigh met her plaint. "Yes, Leyley, we can't keep old Shepherd Finlay from heading out with his flock, and they have to be out and about early. I know it's not what we'd like, but 'a good wizard goes where and when she's needed', and he must need us pretty badly to have gone down to the village yesterday to talk with your Papa. He almost *never* comes down except for market days, and even then not all that often." She walked along for a good while before taking a deep breath and continuing. She could see her daughter stumbling a little, and anything that kept her attention would help. "So, Apprentice, what do we know about the situation?"

Leyla looked up at her for a moment, just blinking, before shaking her head and replying slowly. "Well, Papa said that Shepherd Finlay said that his dog had fought off a wolf that had gone after a lost sheep, but the wolf had hurt his dog's…" She scrunched up her face, trying to remember. "Right foreleg?"

Hannah nodded, and Leyla continued.

"Right foreleg. It hadn't gotten infected, but his dog couldn't keep up, and he needed to have the dog better again soon because… Mama, I'm sorry, I can't remember *why* he couldn't just let his dog get better." She frowned, looking down at the path. "Doesn't seem very *nice* to make your dog keep working after fighting off a *wolf*…"

Her mother's voice was a bit more tart than it might have been if the conversation had taken place a few hours later. "Because the sheep still have to eat, and they're brainless enough to get lost *with* a sheepdog guiding them, so he needs all the help he can get. *Nice* doesn't enter into it, and it's not our place to judge on such things, Apprentice."

Leyla's voice was subdued. "I'm sorry, Wizard Hannah. Um, I think Papa said that the tendons weren't too badly hurt, but they *are* hurt, and the muscle is all torn up. The bones are okay, so we just have to focus on the muscles and tendons."

Hannah nodded. "That about sums it up, Apprentice. Now, let's go through the sheepdog spells…" And if going through the full list of spells, again, was at least half to keep them both awake while they walked, then no harm done.

An hour later, when the sun was almost ready to crest the hills, they were no longer squinting at the increasing light and were able to enjoy the heady scent of the heather as it carpeted the moor, leaving striations of purple scattered with white as far as the eye could see.

The path led up the hillock to a rambling house which might once have started as a simple cottage, but had since grown the way a half-tended garden might. Order in some places gave way to pure perplexment in others, but it certainly looked lived in.

And it suited perfectly the gnarled man who stood out front, puffing a pipe. His shock of white hair stood at all angles, and his clothes were so mismatched that Leyla was convinced that he must have taken them from half a dozen other men. He took one last puff as he saw them, and then a raspy voice reached them. "You're late. Already delayed too long, won't have 'em back in the pen before sundown now. Probably lose half a dozen to the night and wolves, 'specially without Sam."

Hannah inclined her head, slightly. "Apologies, Shepherd Finlay, it took longer than I expected walking in the dark. We're here now, though. If you want to introduce us to Sam then you can be off." She knew there was no point in getting into fine distinctions of things like "before dawn" with old Finlay.

He harrumphed, put his pipe back in his mouth, and without even a gesture turned to walk back inside. Hannah silently motioned to Leyla and they followed him, taking their boots off and putting them in the little entry nook before heading farther inside. A cheerful fire in a rambling room redolent with oily lanolin greeted them, feeling very cosy after the damp chill of the morning. Finlay stood with an unreadable expression, looking down at an old dog with perked-up ears, who greeted them with a canine grin and happily wagging tail. "Now, Sam, this is Wizard Hannah…" The old shepherd gestured first to one, then the other, while Sam's nose snuffled in each direction. "And this is Wizard Apprentice Leyla. They're here to take a look at your leg and see if'n there's something to be done to make you *useful* again."

His face was sour, looking over at them, while Leyla was staring down and almost shaking with outrage. "Better be something, paying for all this firewood, *three* blankets, extra food, wizards and all. Blasted dog's going to ruin me if this keeps up. Now, I'm off. Sam won't bite. Be back an hour, maybe two, after sundown." He waved, seeing Hannah start to speak. "Yes, yes, I paid the extra to Ciaran and all, worth it not to waste any *more* time on this miserableness."

He bit down on his pipe once more, put his boots back on, and strode out. They could hear other dogs running up to him with a few short whistles, before they all moved out of hearing range. Hannah idly scratched behind Sam's ears, just waiting for…

"How could he be so mean to *his own dog?*" Leyla wrapped her arms around the dog in question, putting her angry energy to use in scritches that sent Sam's tail wagging faster. "I don't know why you're so *calm*, Mama."

Hannah just smiled at her daughter's accusing voice. "Because you were listening to his words, and I was listening to his actions." She patted Sam one last time, and started carefully unwrapping the bandages to get a better look at the injured leg. "Look at how many blankets are on his bed, and how many are on Sam's. Think about how hard it is to get firewood up here, and how he's leaving the hearth burning just for Sam. Finlay makes as much by selling trained sheep-dogs as he does anything with his sheep, and if he doesn't have two other dogs that could lead his sheep with their eyes closed, I'll eat my hat. He hired a wizard, but he knows a few spells for his sheep and his dogs, of course, so why would he ask for us?"

She grinned a little at Leyla's wide eyes. "And…think about how happy Sam was when we came in. Dogs know when they're being mistreated, and Sam's not showing any-thing like that. Always worth remembering, paying attention to what people *do,* Ley-ley. But now, let's take a look…"

She gave a low whistle, and Leyla winced, as the last bandage peeled away. Sam gave a low whine, twitching her leg back a little from the pain. "Mm…Finlay got them knit-ted up, but those tendons are definitely strained, and there's still a lot missing." Leyla kept softly petting Sam's back, trying to help soothe the injured dog.

"And she's an old girl, too, her body's struggling…hm. We have her name, Finlay left the stencil out for us. I think the standard strengthening spell, of course, and…" Her eyes grew abstracted as she trailed off.

Leyla just waited, knowing her mother would come out of it eventually.

"Ye-es…strength, injury ward, he's already got poul-tices for the pain, and then the massage spell. Can you tell me why that one, Ley-ley?"

Her daughter nodded. "I think so, Mama. Is that for the tendons, to help them from getting too stiff?"

"It is, very good! Now, help me rewrap this, and we can get to work on the spell."

An hour or so later, they realised what the difficulty was going to be. "Mama…all these have to be *on* Sam, right?

But…the spell's going to be pretty large, how are we going to *fit* it all?"

Hannah glared down at the spellscript. They had a perfectly functional spell that would do everything they needed, and it wouldn't use up more energy than Sam could spare (though she'd need to eat quite a bit more than usual), but…

"Frost and flood. The spell won't work just where she sleeps or anything, it has to be touching her all the time, and that's just not going to fit on a sweater. Even Rosie couldn't make it *that* small."

Leyla looked dubious, too focused and disheartened to pay attention to her mother's cursing. "Aunt Rosie *is* pretty good, but…"

They both shook their heads. Hannah ran a hand through her hair, letting out a puff of air. "Well, now we earn our keep. Let's see how we can cut this down!" She started rearranging the stencils, tracing out different designs with her chalk, absentmindedly fending off an inquisitive snuffly nose from a curious Sam.

The next few hours helped, a little.

Sometimes, they made progress. "Okay, Mama, we don't *actually* need the full name, we can trim these bits out and it doesn't really matter, since she'll be wearing it."

Frequently, they figured out how *not* to make the spell. "Hm…Ley-ley, we're not going to be able to use the other legs like we hoped; the additional script to specify *which* leg takes more room than it saves. With people you've got more room for spellscript than dogs…"

Leyla nodded uncertainly, and Hannah couldn't blame her. This was difficult even for an experienced wizard.

Sam was more of a distraction than anything else. Though, Hannah privately admitted, there were worse ways of being distracted than by a friendly sheepdog demanding belly rubs and snuggling up with fire-warmed fur. And Leyla certainly enjoyed playing with Sam whenever the spellwork was too frustrating.

It wasn't until they were eating from Ciaran's basket that Hannah suddenly stopped mid-bite, making Leyla grin as she had to reach up and rescue the rest of her mother's half-loaf of nutty dark bread from a *very* interested Sam. Well… most of the bread. Leyla told herself Sam needed the extra food anyway, with all the testing they had been doing, and steadfastly ignored the fact that they had a whole pile of scraps for just that purpose.

Eventually, Hannah's eyes refocused with a triumphant laugh. "Hah! *Two* sweaters! Don't know why that didn't occur to me before. The strength and injury ward spells should fit, and the massage and ward spells should fit, and even the most active sheepdog isn't running around *all* day. Strength for running around, massage whenever they stop for a while… Old Finlay will have to switch them, but Sam is *such a good* girl that I'm sure that won't be too bad."

Leyla considered for a moment. "They'll get awfully muddy, Mama. And that's more chances for Sam's nails to catch on the weave. Would Shepherd Finlay be careful enough?"

Her mother shrugged helplessly. "I don't know, but I don't have any other ideas. If those tendons don't get massaged regularly, they'll stiffen up and Sam won't be able to keep up, not with as much hurt as they've already taken. Let's put the spells together and then we can see if it works, at least in theory. Scrub off the test blanket and we can give it a try."

They set to work, and a couple of hours later had workable spells in hand. "That should work, Mama. Sam'll have to eat…twice as much? About twice as much as usual, for a week or so, then once the injury is mostly healed and she doesn't need the injury ward, maybe half again as much as usual. She'll still need two sweaters, though, Mama."

Hannah winced. "Aye, but at least a good bit of the script is the same. Rosie might be able to do one in a couple of days since Sam's already got one sweater, maybe three days for the other? Can pick out the linking spell to the injury ward once that's healed, easy enough. Have to check with her, see if she could set aside what's she's currently working on, but even if we could get the first one done, Sam here could be up and around."

Leyla nodded, but her face was still scrunched up. "But that all costs, Mama. Is he going to want to pay that much? I know you *said* he really cared"—and clearly, Leyla was still not completely convinced—"but you could just buy a new dog for all this." She held onto Sam protectively, clearly not liking her own point.

Her mother looked over at the fire thoughtfully. "I think so, Ley-ley. We'll see… But I think so. And now, *I* need a nap. We're going to be getting home awfully late and it's been a long day." She *very* carefully did not suggest that Leyla might want to consider a nap, knowing better after what had happened when they were keeping an eye on the Martins' garden the other week.

Besides, Sam looked to be settling in for her own rest, and without the novelty of a dog to play with, she thought Leyla would realise how tired she was pretty soon.

A few hours later, they heard barks approaching, and Leyla reluctantly relinquished her new friend as they stood to tell Shepherd Finlay what they had been able to do. He made his way in, pipe no longer in sight, and even before he started taking his boots off his eyes flicked to Sam and then to them.

"Well?"

Hannah gestured to the chalked-out designs. "Shepherd Finlay, I think we have a good solution for you. Sam'll need two sweaters at first, both of which will keep her from hurting herself further. The first will help her stay strong while she goes with you, and the second will help massage her tendons so they don't get too stiff, regardless of how mucky she might get. Eventually, she—"

Finlay snorted. "Bah, don't see why I'd go to the trouble of all that. Just need her out keeping the sheep in line. Didn't lose any today, but that was pure luck, and I don't trust luck."

Hannah frowned. "The massaging is important, otherwise she'll—"

He gestured sharply, irritated. "I know better than you why it's important, aye, but I can massage her myself, and damn the muck anyhow. Hands wash, and I've done worse for less. How much more feeding will she need, then?"

Leyla piped up. "Shepherd Finlay, about twice as much, until she's healed more, then maybe half again. But that'll have to be for a while, maybe forever."

Finlay grunted, setting his boots up and then heading over to stand by Sam, whose wagging tail and nuzzling left her feelings clear. "Aye, that I can manage. When can I get the spell, then?"

Both their eyebrows rose at his not protesting the food at all. "I'll have to check with Rosie, but I'm hoping two or three days."

He grunted again, glaring down at Sam. "You hear that, you mangy mongrel? Be the better part of a week with you lounging around, all said and done! If I had a good leader for the pack then I wouldn't have to put up with this foolishness. But I don't, so we'll just have to make do until one or the other of us keels over."

Sam's tail never stopped wagging, though she winced a bit as she shifted around to start licking his other foot.

"Well, what's done is done. Thankee, Wizard Hannah, and I'll look for that sweater on market day then." He nodded sharply and clearly dismissed them from his attention, going to an old, sturdy chair. His joints creaked audibly as he moved it over by the pile of blankets Sam was resting in.

Hannah just shook her head, smiling, and she and Leyla put their boots on and began the walk home, which didn't seem quite as long as the way there had been. She didn't think it was just because of the difference in the hour, either.

It was dark enough that the peaty smell and pleasant trickling of the brook that ran past their house was the first sign that they had nearly reached their destination, before they turned up the lane and could see the gleaming firelight. They were both yawning again by the time they were racking up their walking sticks, though, and the warm house was even more cheerful than usual as Ciaran carried the empty basket away.

"And how was old Finlay? He seemed less irascible than usual when he came by yesterday."

Leyla paused for a thoughtful moment, and Ciaran looked over in surprise at the silence. "I thought we was very mean, at first, Papa. But now…" She looked over at her mother. "I think his *actions* say he's *actually* a very nice man."

Ciaran's brows rose as he looked over at his wife, who had a smug, if tired, look on her face. "Then I'd say you've learned more about him than most of the village, little Nightstar. And you were able to help poor Sam out?"

Hannah nodded as she warmed her hands gratefully by the fire. "That we did, just need to get this spell over to Rosie in the morning. Should have her leading the pack again in a few days."

Ciaran smiled. "Then you did a good day's work. Now, I have some special dumplings tonight, I think you'll enjoy them. And, my wonderful ladies—"

He wrapped them both up in a big hug, and they could feel his resonant voice as much as hear it.

"Welcome home."

The Devil in the Details

Hannah and Leyla were running.

Normally, Hannah would be able to outpace her daughter easily, but she was carrying her heavy emergency pack, and still struggling to get it seated, and Leyla had gone ahead while her mother was still putting her boots on after they heard. Hannah's nerves were jangling as they turned the corner, and Leyla's gasps for air were sharp whistles, but thankfully they did not have much farther to go. The man on lookout spotted them and shouted in strangled almost-relief, sprinting towards them and nearly ripping the pack off Hannah before turning and picking up Leyla to help them move just that little bit faster.

Hannah's rangy legs loped ahead of them, and she didn't have to guess where in the camp to go as the shouts rang out when they saw the wizard arrive. She nearly barrelled into a sturdy man with a thick black beard, but the man just looked ready to catch her if she needed it, and he more or less shoved her toward the cot trying to direct her. Hannah could hear Leyla's still-gasping breaths approaching, but all that meant right now was her bag would be here in moments. And as she took in the scene…

Not good. The man on the cot was unconscious, which was at least a blessing, and they had gotten the emergency charcoal ready for whatever spellwork she needed to do, but those were the *only* good signs. He was older, and not quite as hale as the woodcutters and charcoal burners who made up this camp usually were. She tried to estimate how much blood he had lost already, but the pile of gory fabric next to him and the slowly-growing morass of mud defied a guess other than "too much." They had a tourniquet on his leg, but while that might have helped for the original slash, the new puncture wounds went up and down the whole length of the leg, and the wounds above the band were still bleeding heavily despite the pressure.

And less mortally urgent but no less serious, there was a younger man on another cot shivering with what was clearly spellshakes, as his body tried to make up the heat drained to power the botched spell. She would focus on him later, and prayed it wouldn't be a *lifetime* later.

The man arrived with her bag, and she quickly pulled out her longest bandage, tearing it out of its oilcloth wrapping in her haste, and examined it while she unrolled it for ten agonising heartbeats, with pulses of blood onto the dirt as her clock since the last cloths had soaked through. Finding no fault in the pattern, she shouldered aside the caretakers and wrapped it around the entire leg, making sure none of the deep holes were uncovered, and out of the corner of one eye saw Leyla holding the power ribbon as she moved to the charcoal pile. Panic nearly strangled her, but she managed a shrill cry. "Ley, *gloves!*"

Her daughter gulped, face growing pale under her flush, and started fumbling for her gloves, before one of the nearby folk took the ribbon from her and held it down to the pile with his own gloved hand. Hannah bit back a sob of barely-avoided horror, and fastened the last bit of spellscript together with the hook. The charcoal roared in a blast of heat before turning into ash in a bare instant, almost every last inch of it used to supply the energy for the spell, and the man under her hands bucked and woke with a scream as the punctures closed in a moment of agony.

Hannah undid the hook, unwrapped the leg, and handed the bandage off to Leyla (and she *could not* think about Leyla right now, or she would just start screaming) as she began inspecting, seeing if there was anything missed. The skin over where the punctures had been was red and raw looking, but whole, and she was about to sigh in relief when a panicked call of *"Wizard!"* rang out from someone nervously watching the other cot.

The man with spellshakes had gone from shivers to convulsions, and Hannah swore, slipping in the blood-mud as she scrambled to get to him. She whipped her head around, her night-braid flying from the suddenness of it, but all she really needed to see was the ashen expressions on a few faces to know she had already burned their entire emergency store. She swore again with feeling, and quickly pointed at three of the burliest and heavyset men.

"You, you, you, here! Ley-ley, powershare spell!"

Leyla started rooting through the bag, as the three men gathered close around their convulsing workmate, and Hannah gave firm orders. "We need to get him warmed inside again, and we're doing it the hard way. You, hands to chest; you, hands to arms; and you, hands to legs. Kneel down, you're going to about keel over when—"

"Here, Mama, the spell!"

The two wrapped the intricate spell-scarf in three broad loops, tying each man to their dying friend, and Hannah hooked the spell together with steady hands, though the rest of her shook. All three slumped, one falling completely over, and at first Hannah was terrified there was something *else* wrong as the convulsions got worse. She started examining him further, cursing once more. "Damnit, I'm a wizard, not a doctor! Where's one of those blasted cityfolk when you need one?"

She was looking through her pack again, trying to bludgeon her brain into remembering the season she'd spent with that travelling sawbones and what *else* caused convulsions when they finally started slowing and the man started moaning. Which, normally, would be a cause for concern, but right now made her jump for joy that he had that much control of his lungs again. Well, get up on her toes with joy—jumping was a bit dicey at the moment with all the muck and tumbled men about.

Hannah spent a tense few minutes going back and forth between the two cots, and doing a few more cautious reinforcement spells powered by a few volunteers, before finally they both *seemed* at least to be resting in something that might be sleep, and not in immediate danger of dropping dead or jumping about or some other nonsense she couldn't think of right now. She collapsed onto a fresh stump someone had (mostly) sanded down, and lay flat on her back with her arms dangling for a moment, just breathing and settling.

After a time, Leyla came and flopped across her and Hannah whuffed at the impact before curling an arm around her. "*That* was a job and a half—and no mistake, little Nightstar, we've earned our bread today."

Leyla nodded into her mother's shoulder, silent still for the time being. They could hear the sounds of people starting to clean up the messes and pulling some kind of order from the wreckage about them, but they were both content to let that happen, for a bit. Or, as Hannah's twinging back and sore neck protested, maybe *more* than a bit as they woke from their nap to see the sturdy man with the black beard from before. Now that she wasn't in a tearing hurry, Hannah could recognise Liam Bain, who might have been the leader of the camp, or might just have been the one who kept everyone organised, depending on who you asked.

"Wizards, we're just fixing to have a midday meal, figured you might want to join us for that. I know you've got some rations in that bag of yours, but if I recall aright from when you spent that day with us a few seasons back, they'nt particularly tasty."

Hannah could smell that he was certainly right—whatever they were making was better than her field pemmican.

"Good thinking and appreciated, Liam. My little apprentice gets a mite cranky when she hasn't eaten, so this will help us make it home with my hair still attached to my head."

Leyla made a face at this mildly insulting (though not incorrect) aspersion on her character, and wriggled her way free so she could follow her nose in a huff.

Hannah sighed, as she knew standing up with the way her back felt was going to be rough, and gladly accepted an armclasp from Liam to make it upright.

"Oof, going to be feeling that for a bit. I assume from you letting us sleep they're both still managing?"

"Aye, that they are, Wizard, that they are. And right glad we are of it too. When old Thomas's leg took that bad axe swing, it didn't look good to begin with. But when young Angus did the sewing spell to fix it up and it all went horrible wrong, well, I don't mind telling you that I didn't think he was…well. And Angus was in no good state either—never seen the spellshakes as bad as that. Plain enough to see why, though, as many holes as ended up in his uncle's leg."

A somewhat ragged cheer rose ahead, and they both grinned as they saw Leyla getting picked up by a boisterous man and spun around a bit before they let her take a seat. Another cheer greeted Hannah when she was noticed, and a lot of "if it hadn't been for you" and "sharp as a whistle and quick as a snake, that's what it was" followed, while the two wizards were showered in food and drink. It wasn't fancy, and the sharp scent of pine resin permeated it all, but it was hot and hearty and most importantly *plenty*, which suited everyone around the table well enough.

Conversation, by mutual unspoken agreement, stayed away from how awful the day nearly had been, aside from a couple of times when Leyla would start to ask a question before being distracted with some japery from one corner or another. But, eventually, the meal ended, and Hannah winced as she stood up from the rough-hewn bench and stretched.

"Yep, still feeling it…well. Time to go see the spell that went wrong, Apprentice. I've a guess on how a sewing spell went like that, but I've never seen it happen, and we should be able to piece it together quickly enough."

Leyla nodded quietly and soberly, and then went to go find the spellcloth. It had been flung a little way off, and was tangled up on a few tree roots, but was easy enough to disentangle. Then, they went to work. The blood and dirt stains didn't help any, but they found the problem fairly quickly even so.

"Now, how in the great green wood did something *nibble* this?"

Hannah's voice was incredulous, and Leyla's was too. "Weren't they *storing* their *spells* properly? Mama, should we look at the rest of them?"

Hannah nodded back, looking momentarily stricken and horrified. It was plain enough, now. Something had chewed through a bit of the linen, and one of the whorls it had gone through had been the one that connected an entire section of the spell. In essence, it had converted from a *sewing* spell, designed to suture together any open wound (and with some handy catgut attached to one end of the spellcloth, now thoroughly mauled) to a *puncturing* spell which poked holes through anything it touched. If something had gotten in to any of the other spells...

They tracked down Liam, who was helping clean the branches off a felled log, and when they told him what they found he blanched and hurriedly showed them where the emergency spells were stored. On the far corner of the box they found a small gap, and while most of the spells seemed untouched in their oilcloths, a few more had been gnawed at, though in only one other case had whatever it was gone past the oilcloth to the spell itself.

Liam sighed. "Add it to the tale of the day, I suppose. Shoring up the box, replacing two spells, two men down, emergency bin to be refilled, and we just need to be more careful. We might as well have been *freehanding* it, being this careless!"

Leyla's eyes were wide at hearing that kind of language, and the woodcutter winced and ducked his head apologetically to Hannah, who waved her forgiveness. She didn't *disagree*, after all.

He sucked his teeth a moment. "Think we need a bigger emergency bin, after this, need the power available if we get another bad accident. Going to be a lean few seasons…"

Despite his words, a warm smile grew on his face. "But we'd all rather a lean season or three than losing two of our own. Thankee again, Wizards. It's right glad I am that you came, and we'll settle up with Ciaran soonest." The woodcutter gave them a friendly nod, and began striding back towards the log. "Ollie! Stop lazing about, don't you know we've got a whole passel of spellwork to pay for?"

Hannah and Leyla waved to everyone, gathered up a few odds and ends, and went on their way. They were quiet for a good while as they walked, enjoying the warm afternoon sun and the light breeze. But eventually Leyla spoke up, with a questioning tone. "Mama, it seems like they had an *awful* lot of bad luck, all at once…?"

Her mother gave a grim smile back. "Does it, now? Liam wasn't wrong, they *were* careless. You saw me checking my spell even while that man Thomas was bleeding out, because you *have* to, or…you get that."

Leyla just said, very quietly, "Oh." They walked on for a while longer, before she spoke again. "I…need to be more careful, then. With my gloves."

Hannah nodded, slowly, as if she was afraid that a sudden movement would break through a fragile wall holding back a river. And before she could master her not-blocked-enough memory of terror, they saw the house up ahead. Ciaran must have caught sight of them too, as the door opened and he strode down the lane.

"I was hoping you would be home soon. They sent word that Thomas and Angus were both going to survive not too much worse for the wear..." He trailed off in concern at the look of suppressed anguish on Hannah's face, and he changed tack. "Leyla, I made treats for you both today, and if you hurry, you can pick which flavour of pie you want."

Leyla perked up at the mention of treats and dashed ahead, her cares forgotten for the moment. Hannah was not quite so lucky, and she fell into Ciaran's arms, clutching at him. "Oh, *Cirie*, she almost...I almost completed a spell while she was holding it... It burned a *whole bin,* Ciaran, if she'd still been touching..."

"Shh, shh, it's all right, it's all right my love. You didn't, and she didn't. It's all right, it's all right." He squeezed her tightly for a long, long moment, while the shudders subsided. And eventually, Hannah breathed in sharply and stood up, wiping at her face and forcing a smile.

"So, pies, is it? I knew I married you for a reason..."

Ciaran knew that they would talk more, later, but for now he just settled an arm around her and led her inside. "More than one, I hope! But I *do* make an excellent pie, if I do say so myself. And, both of you..." He pitched his voice to reach inside, to where they could hear a child eagerly juggling a too-hot pie.

"Welcome home."

The Hunter in the Treehouse

Leyla swung her heels back and forth at the table. "It's nice seeing Papa before we leave, isn't it?" She dipped a bit of yesterday's bread in her hot broth, looking over at her mother through the steam wreathing her face as she nibbled.

Hannah gave a warm smile. "Yes, it is. Nice enough to wish he'd see us off every day!" Her tone was teasing, and she could guess how he'd respond.

"If you left at a *civilised* hour every day, then I would be *happy* to break my fast with you. But otherwise, I will be enjoying my rest, thank you." Ciaran gave an overwrought sniff, making Leyla giggle, before he grinned and kissed the top of Hannah's head on his way to the pot to fill up his own mug.

"It's not every day that we're doing luxury work, more's the pity, but it's nice to enjoy it while we can." Hannah leaned her head back to catch her husband as he moved back to the table, and closed her eyes for a moment as his fingers traced a strand of hair from her temple to the nape of her neck. "Mmm…*definitely* nice to enjoy it…"

"Well, if Lukas likes your work, you might end up getting more like this. He's got plenty of friends in town, after all his years of trading, and you know the Wizard's Guild there always overbuilds their spells." Ciaran seated himself, tearing up his own bread into bite-sized chunks before he began dipping it.

Hannah tore off a hunk of her loaf with her teeth, chewing strenuously on the broth-soaked bread while she nodded at Ciaran. He rolled his eyes dramatically before stage-whispering to Leyla, "*Barbarian*." Leyla's dimples showed as she stifled another giggle while Hannah's put-upon affront combined with the big bite to make her look like an outraged chipmunk.

But, eventually, they made their way out the door. The crisp autumn air made them happy for the warm breakfast, and they pointed out especially interesting colours in the falling leaves to each other, and debated the merits of whether red or yellow was the superior shade, before agreeing that orange had the best of both worlds, even better than the evergreen pine needles. They saw plenty of signs of life beside the path from darting swallows chasing flies to curious squirrels, as this was far from where the loggers worked and not many came through here besides the foragers, occasional young lovers looking for some privacy, and, of course…

Thunk!

They both jumped at the sudden noise, and saw well ahead of them an old bit of deadwood with a quarrel sticking out of it. As they approached, more cautiously now, a boisterous voice called out.

"Hallo, mistress and miss! Don't mind me, just taking advantage of the time for a little target practice!" A man strode out, shortish and a bit heavyset, but nimble and with long fingers splayed as he waved a cheerful greeting, before starting to carefully work the bolt free. "Got a good kill earlier, and with all the blood and ruckus, not to mention whatever you fine ladies get up to, I suspect there won't be much else coming around anytime soon." He finished retrieving the bolt, inspecting it carefully for any damage, then placed it into a small hip quiver alongside a few companions before offering a handclasp.

Hannah nodded respectfully as she took it, and Leyla offered up a curious "Was that a good shot, Mister Robertson?" which made him grin broadly, and not at the polite honorific.

"Well now, little miss, it was an excellent shot! Best shot I've managed in a week, split this little mushroom right in two! Of course, I was *aiming* for this flower on the other side, you see, but any shot that gets the kill, eh?" He chuckled self-deprecatingly, and Leyla's smile grew broader. "Now, as I understand it, your Ciaran gave you the basics, yes?"

The rangy wizard nodded. "Aye, you've got a hunting blind that you wanted made a little less obtrusive. Less noise, less scent, that sort of thing."

"Right you are! Now, I understand you two are the clever ones, so I won't tell you how to do your jobs, but I'm not the quietest man around and I do enjoy my venison, as does the missus, so anything that'll help us with that will be just the thing. I'll take you to it, answer any questions you might have, and then go back to my target practice so as to be out of your hair." He set off away from the path, pausing only to snatch up the crossbow he had left leaning against a tree, and they all made their way deeper into the forest.

Hannah and Leyla were at first inclined to be silent while they walked, not certain what Lukas would prefer, but he soon had them laughing at various jests and wheedled out of them what they had discussed on the earlier leg of their journey before wading into the debate with gusto. He opined that the *brown* leaves were the best, in defiance of all convention, because they turned the same shade as some kinds of wood and, after all, what could make better sense than trees making leaves which turned the same colour as the trees?

"And besides, I'm a man of fashion, or so my tailor tells me, and would it be right for me to be outdressed by a *tree*, I ask you?"

Leyla grinned up at him before daring a "Your tailor might think so, because then you'd have to go see him again!"

Lukas gave a deep belly laugh as he clapped. "Ah, now you've figured me out! The missus wouldn't approve, though—she'd say I'm too much of a clotheshorse as it is. Of course, I always say that I can't be a clothes-*horse*, as I'm clearly a clothes-*ox*!"

Leyla's giggles joined his own self-amused laughter, and Hannah just shook her head while she grinned and chuckled. So while it was a ways to the hunting blind, it felt like no time at all before they arrived.

The blind was cleverly disguised in a tree, spreading its weight across a few sturdy branches as well as the trunk itself. Lukas grabbed a long hanging hook, and with a practised hand caught the rope ladder at the top and tipped it to fall towards them. "There we go! It's a bit of an extravagance, I'll admit, but as much as I love venison I spend a fair amount of time up here, and I thought I might as well make the most of it!"

Leyla's eyes had gone wide as she took it all in, and her awed voice was soft, almost reverent. "Mister Robertson… this isn't a hunting blind…"

He tilted his head back at her, quizzically. "If it's not, then I think I've been mighty confused for a few years now, but—"

"It's a treehouse!"

His mouth opened into an understanding "O," before he began chuckling again. "Well, now, I can hardly argue with that! A treehouse indeed, and me none the wiser all these years! Wizard Hannah, I see that the apple doesn't fall far from the tree, nor indeed the treehouse, you've got a bright young girl there, that you do!"

Hannah was poorly hiding her snickers at the whole interplay, and she watched with tolerant amusement as her daughter scampered up the rope ladder before she followed. "I think you may have a new best friend, Trader Lukas. The last time I saw her that excited was the day she used her first real spell."

Lukas led the rear and pulled the ladder up after them, still chuckling. "I can hardly blame her! Don't know how I never thought about it, all these years, but I'd certainly have sold any three of the lads I grew up with for my own treehouse, provided they came by to admire it properly afterwards, of course." His beaming grin took in the young apprentice dashing back and forth, examining every nook and cranny, leaning over the edges to peer down at the forest floor, and drumming her feet with excitement.

Hannah gauged Lukas's mood, and let Leyla run around for a couple of minutes more while they talked desultorily about a few details, before finally calling out a firm "Apprentice." Her daughter stopped guiltily and made her way back to the adults.

"Sorry, Wizard Hannah, Mister Robertson!"

Lukas just kept grinning as he tipped his hat. "Nothing to apologise to me about, little miss, but I'll be on my way now and leave you two to it! Or, as one of the birdies around here might say, 'too-tooit'!" Chuckling at his own jest, he let the rope ladder down and made his way to the forest floor with his crossbow, heading off to, as he put it to Hannah, "see how many more mushrooms I can split while I aim at flowers!"

"Now, Apprentice, time to actually earn our keep. Just like we talked about, let's start with the charcoal."

Leyla nodded and started rummaging through the bulky (though oddly light) pack her mother had carried out today in addition to her usual spell supplies. First was a double-sided wooden bin, filled with charcoal. Ciaran had done the spell-work on the outside of the inner wall, and it was now safely protected against bumps and most other damage by the outer wall as well as proper sealing. It wouldn't last forever, but the worst that would happen if *this* spell was damaged would be that everything would start to smell like charcoal, and it was much, much cheaper to replace the box every decade or two (even assuming replacement was needed) than to make something similar out of metal.

They had a small debate about where to place it, before eventually deciding that the bottom of the crossbow rack was as close as made no difference to the centre of the place. Next to this, they placed most of the rest of the pack, after extracting a couple dozen small wooden plaques. They next tied the pack to the bin, carefully making sure that the straps were not straining as everything settled.

Then, they started nailing up the plaques, each inscribed with a linking spell, all over the structure, using the already-drilled holes so as not to interfere with the spellwork. What followed next was testing with their usual marked pieces of wood, various odoriferous materials for the scent-trapping spells, and loud noises for the sound-dampening spells, making sure that each component of the system worked as intended and that the power draw of the spells wasn't more than they had calculated.

All told, they were at it for a few hours, but most of that was the testing. So by the time Lukas returned, they had already eaten the hand pies Ciaran had packed for them, and Leyla was back to treating the treehouse like her own personal playground while Hannah napped. He called out for the rope ladder, which Leyla eagerly lowered for him, and he popped his head up with what was clearly his usual grin.

"Well, I can see a few things are different already! Everything went well then, I take it?"

Hannah was on her feet by this time, and she gave a mischievous grin of her own. "Rather than taking our word for it, I think you should test it, Trader Lukas. We put the power linkage here, thought a hat would be easy enough for you to put on for it, and you could put it on different hats easily enough if you wanted."

She handed over a broad-brimmed hat, and he took it a bit cautiously. "Oh, *I'm* powering it, am I? Well, I don't mean to second-guess you, Wizard, but I'm not exactly the most strapping man around. Keeping a spell going *while* hunting seems a bit much to ask of a trader."

Hannah just kept grinning. "Trader Lukas, all I ask is that you try it. If it's too much of a draw, then I'll redo the spells to pull from a charcoal bin, free of charge."

Lukas's brows rose. "Well, Wizard Hannah, you certainly said the magic words in *my* line of business! Let's give this a try, then." He gingerly lowered it on to his head, and waited for a moment. "Ah, what do I need to do to have it start, then?"

Hannah's grin broadened. "It's already running."

"Good grief, Wizard! That's *it?* I'm not even feeling a tickle!"

Hannah waggled her hand back and forth. "Well, you won't yet. If you leave it on for a whole day, you'll probably feel like you walked another mile or two than you actually did, but that should be about it."

Lukas stared with some amazement, and more caution. "That's a hefty accomplishment, if it does everything we talked about."

Leyla piped up. "Oh, I think we can show that! Mister Robertson, look!" The young apprentice pulled out a stinkbug and squished it, giggling a little at the ickiness of it. Lukas recoiled at first, reaching for his nose…and then stopped, jaw falling open.

"What in the blue blazes? I don't smell a thing! But the Guild smell-stoppers, they burn through wood on the regular!"

Hannah's lips quirked. "That's because they're getting rid of the smell entirely—which is maybe good in a big town for big stenches, I can't say, but out here, all you need is for it to not reach anything you might be hunting, right? So instead…" She tapped on the charcoal bin, and opened it up. "It all goes here. Now, you'll have to replace the charcoal every so often, maybe once a season, more if you're hitting more flowers than mushrooms, but it'll burn just fine once it's soaked up as much as it'll handle. Have to use the medicinal charcoal, mind, not just the regular stuff, but the cost'll be way less than powering the Guild spell."

The trader shook his head slowly. "Well, I'll be. Never would have thought of it. Stuff just eats the smells right up, that it does, helps keep the air clear when the doctors are working. I've seen that before. And the sound?"

Leyla spoke up again. "Mister Robertson, would you say I could yell pretty loudly if I wanted to?"

Lukas laughed. "That I would, Apprentice Leyla, that I would!"

"Then I'll take the hat, and if you want to go a little ways from the tree, I'm going to yell as *loud* as I can, and we'll see what you hear!"

He handed it over wordlessly and began making his way down the ladder, still shaking his head. Leyla waited until he stopped a few yards away from the tree and waved before she took in a deep breath, and started bellowing as best she could. Hannah watched with amusement as Lukas's astonished face looked up at them, and he scurried back up the ladder.

"Phew! Keep doing that and I'll be fitter than a fiddle in no time. I heard you, right enough, but only just! How in the world did you manage that?"

"The same way as the scents, Trader Lukas. See, this pack here..." Hannah opened it up, showing it to be stuffed with rags and bits of fluff. "All the sounds in the blind get bounced around in this before they head back out. And moving just the little bits of air that need to be cleaned, and the sounds that need to be deadened, takes not much power at all. You could clean a whole deer here and the blood scent wouldn't get out, and the carving wouldn't disturb anything past ten yards or so."

He just laughed again, not stopping for a good bit. "Seems Lachlan wasn't just selling me on his brother's wife, that was just the sober truth. Wizards, I'm mighty obliged, and your services would be cheap at twice the price. I'll be sure to spread that around, too, and I think Ciaran will be happy when I come to settle up." He offered a handclasp again, both to Hannah and Leyla, and leaned down to Leyla as she shook his arm vigorously with both hands.

"Now, Leyla, word to the wise… I mostly only hunt in autumn, maybe a bit at the end of summer. And if someone wanted a nice treehouse to enjoy in other seasons, as long as everything was all cleaned up and tidy by the time I arrived, well, you know that Lukas Robertson, he couldn't see the forest for the trees and he'd be none the wiser about any trespassers, would he?" A finger to the side of his nose and a sly wink met her wide eyes, and she looked up at Hannah for approval.

Hannah, seeing the writing on the wall, sighed and nodded, causing Leyla to leave off on shaking his arm and hug his leg instead. He returned the hug before patting her on the back and straightening.

"Now, I see the sun's getting a mite low, given how far back we all have to walk, and I did promise your father and your husband you'd be back by sundown and all, so we should get moving!"

The walk back didn't feel any longer than the walk out had, as they laughed and joked and told increasingly ridiculous stories (none better than Lukas, who had the advantage of wide travel, though sometimes he started laughing at his own story before he even finished), and he shared one last hug with Leyla and handclasp with Hannah before he turned off to his own home in the village proper. Leyla ran up the path to the house, with Hannah following more sedately (though no less cheerfully), and grinned as Ciaran opened the door to his daughter leaping into him.

"Papa! It worked *so well*, he said he was happy and going to tell everyone and I think he's going to pay you something extra and *I get to use his treehouse* and the stinkbug didn't even stink when I squished it and—"

Ciaran "oof"d at the impact, staggering a moment under the bombardment of squiggly child and barrage of stories, before he managed to get a word in. "Well, that sounds like *quite* the day! You'll have to tell me all about it *after* you wash up for supper."

Hannah made it to the door and gave her husband a warm kiss as Leyla ran inside. "It worked just as well as we'd hoped, and better than I'd have guessed. I don't know how Lachlan convinced him, but we'll have to do something for him."

Ciaran just smiled. "That's what family's for, though I might have been working on a special pie for him and Calvin. But, for now—" He shut the door behind them, and squeezed Hannah back.

"Welcome home."

Interlude: Ciaran

Ciaran finished cleaning up the usual detritus from Hannah and Leyla's rushed (and groggy) breakfast, made sure his pack had everything necessary, and grabbed his finely carved walking stick and somewhat threadbare hat as he set out. He enjoyed, as he always did, the masses of hydrangeas, autumn's joy, and other wild flowers give way to carefully ordered crops as he approached Bywater proper. He knew the flowers gave the farmers a little grief, but he also knew most thought they were worth it. The market day was already in full swing by the time he arrived, and some amused (and envious) calls greeted him.

"Well now, finally sleepyhead comes to grace us with his presence!"

"Ah, midmorning's good enough for the likes of Ciaran now, isn't it?"

"We should be lucky—sometimes it's more like midday afore he gets up, aye?"

Ciaran smiled, a trifle smugly. "Nothing to sell today, so midmorning's plenty of time for what I need to do."

This was greeted with a low whistle and a few raised eyebrows, but it was Eva Nelson who called out, "No stencils for sale today, then, Ciaran-my-lad? Been too busy with commissions, aye?"

Ciaran just smiled more widely as he made his way to the building that housed the village library. Its minder was out front, as usual on a market day, doing brisk business trading various spell stencils around with the market-goers. Ciaran politely waited his turn in the short queue, knowing that quite a few people were keeping half an eye on him, and then pulled several stencils out of his pack and placed them on the little table. And if he did so a trifle ostentatiously, could anyone blame him?

"Here is our contribution to the village library for the year, Librarian Matthew. Half a dozen stencils as usual."

The librarian's eyebrows went up too, and he picked them up with his good hand before using the thumb on his other to trace the pattern on each, carefully avoiding the gap where the stencil omitted the activation line so as not to trigger the spell before saying formally, "And I accept your contribution, Spellbinder Ciaran." He paused a moment before adding, "And a season and a half early, too—that's quite a thing."

Ciaran nodded, grinning now. "Yes, it is. Hannah's been doing very well by us." And as he went about the rest of his business, he kept an ear open for all the murmurs. There had been talk when he and Hannah had married, some wondering why he had risked a match with a landless girl, despite her good showing at every Fair. But today, they should start to see what he had known all along...

"Rosie Hendry, how are you today? Little Tansy and Tyler over that bout of sniffles?"

"Ciaran Hendry, it's a beautiful day, that posset you made for them seemed to help wonders, and I believe I have something for you here, that cloak for Hannah."

Ciaran admired the fine work from his sister-by-marriage, and knew that while Hannah might not notice, it would make more than a little difference in keeping her warm on her rounds this winter. His deep voice showed his approval. "Wonderful! And the one for Leyla should still be ready for next market day? Did there end up being enough cherries in the bushels, or do I owe you anything for that?"

Rosie shook her head, grinning. "More than plenty cherries! I should even be able to put a few stars on for the little Night-star. Tell Calvin and Lachlan those cherries get better every year, and this one's no exception. Wouldn't mind if you did a few more jobs for them, I know you could use a nice Fair-day shirt, and if my apprentices had a few more cherry pies waiting for me that would be a nice thing indeed."

Ciaran laughed. "I'll have to tell them that when next I'm wheeling and dealing with my brother and his husband, then! Have to make sure our best embroiderer is kept in cherry pies, after all."

They gossiped for a time before he spotted Finlay, and made his way over to the old shepherd who was flanked by a tail-wagging Sam in her new sweater, who in turn was keeping her eye on an old ewe.

"Well then, Spellbinder, I'm a man who keeps his word and as you and yours did as asked, I've gotten the last of the wool over to the Embroiderer there for her portion, and this here ewe is yours. She won't last another winter. Mutton'll be tough but plenty of it, plus all the rest."

Ciaran inclined his head to the gnarled shepherd, and they went over to work out the butchering details with Edith. Most of it went to various others in the market, fuel for the little world of barter Ciaran made his living in, but there was still going to be a nice amount of stew meat at the end of it for the family. He shook hands with Edith and Finlay, then made his way to the charcoal burners' wagon as the next on his list.

"Liam Bain, how are Thomas and young Angus doing? Still healing up well? Is Thomas walking again yet?"

The sturdy man tipped his broad-brimmed hat to Ciaran. "Aye, that he is, and that's a marvel itself when all's said and done. Your ladies did a miracle there, Spellbinder, that they did, and we should have the charcoal we promised delivered afore next market day. And as thanks, and to make sure they come running again if we need it, the lasses and lads decided we should cover your village charcoal contribution for the season too, aye."

Ciaran's eyes widened. He knew how much that accident had set them behind, and a season's worth of charcoal was no small thing. "Then on behalf of Hannah and her apprentice, I thank you and yours, and you can be sure they'll come running again if needed."

Liam nodded sombrely, and shook Ciaran's hand before turning to make a deal with Calvin about another delivery to the orchard. Calvin smiled distractedly at Ciaran, and Ciaran waved to indicate he understood. They'd see each other again soon enough, and could catch up on Anabelle's latest achievements then.

"Well, now, Spellbinder! There you are, and I'd say 'at last' except I approve of a man who knows the hours best for him, and it's not as if I can complain about your service! What your ladies did is a marvel and no mistake, good value at twice the price, and I'll be telling all my friends in Meldrum so too."

Ciaran smiled and turned toward the effusive Lukas, accepting the vigorous handshake, and had to struggle to keep from preening as everyone nearby in the market heard the trader count out a satisfying weight of silver coin into Ciaran's hand. Coin wasn't often seen among the villagers themselves, and he could practically hear certain busybodies mulling over what the day's events meant for the place of his family in the village.

"Thank you indeed, Trader Lukas, and we're glad you think so. We'll be happy to do more work for you, or any friends of yours, any time."

A comfortable gossip ensued, with both trading jokes and Lukas's lighter chuckles joining Ciaran's rumbling ones. After that, Ciaran finished up his rounds with everyone, and made his way back home well before sunset with a heavier pack and a lighter heart. They were already much further along the preparations for winter than usual, and he decided a special treat was in order. Hannah and Leyla were overnighting at one of the nearby farms, testing to find where the pest wards were being evaded, and when they dragged themselves back the next day he had no doubt they would be tired and irritable. A treat was just the thing.

The weather should be clear and cold tonight, perfect for this, and he spent the remainder of the afternoon preparing in his outdoor space, lighting the brick oven built in to one wall just before sundown so he could enjoy the sunset. The pies went into the oven first, and he worked well into the night mostly by feel. The various breads and rolls and other nibbles formed under practised hands while he stared up at the night sky, basking in the slow wheel of the constellations. It was worth a few jibes, and Hannah always enjoyed the results of his nighttime baking, not to mention the heat from the oven.

And tomorrow, he would get to see the excited smiles from his wife and daughter when, as always, he welcomed them home.

Housewarming Gifts

Hannah rocked back and forth on her heels while Leyla finished packing their supplies. "I don't know why you had to go and tell Lennox Milligan about house-naming anyhow, Cirie." She stretched and jittered one foot, twisting and untwisting a strand of hair.

Her husband's sleepy voice attempted to be soothing. "Because 'a good wizard always pushes herself to learn how and why,' love, and it was niggling at the back of your head what made it finally work here. And besides, I enjoy bragging about my wife." He set the last loaf in the basket before turning, disentangling her fingers from her hair, and kissing them one by one. "I'm allowed, you know."

A genuine smile stole onto her face, and she leaned up against him before saying, "That you are, aye, that you are."

A deep chuckle rumbled through his chest as she listened to his heartbeat, before he said, "And I even woke up at this *miserable* hour to see you off, knowing you would be like this. So I think I have paid for any imaginary infraction, and you can just focus on your wizardry. And remember: *sundown*, both of you. You won't name that house in a day, and if the words 'Well, maybe if we just try a *little* longer...' cross your lips, I want you to think about *exactly* how grumpy I will be if you are late."

Leyla's voice, muffled by the pack as she double-checked the stencils, came back cheerfully. "Yes, Papa. Don't worry, we'll be back, it's too cold already to want to walk home at night." She clasped the pack, shouldered it, and grabbed the basket. "Ready, Mama?"

Hannah took a deep breath in, a deep breath out, and then reluctantly released her husband and started for the door. "Yes, Ley-ley. As ready as I'll be, anyway." And with a still-yawning farewell from Ciaran following them down the path, they set out. Rae Milligan's house was on the other side of the river, though thankfully not too far from the bridge, and they had a decent walk ahead of them which to Leyla's mind gave plenty of time for questions.

"Wizard Hannah, why *is* it so hard to name houses? We came up with five whole names for Uncle Martin and Uncle Calvin's orchard, and that didn't seem so bad...?"

The question helped Hannah's head stop swirling around what-if's and focus, for which she was grateful. "Well, Apprentice, that's a good question! And if you ever find out the answer, then you'll be famous indeed, for no one's really sure. At least no one I've ever talked to, leastwise, and the mages at the University are always squabbling about it. You'd think that if we knew the names of the bricks and slate, the hearth and the chimney, that'd work just like knowing the trees and the soil, and the water and the light at the orchard. But, somehow, houses aren't quite the same.

And I don't rightly know why it is I was able to find a good name for our house, it just…felt right, when I thought about us and it and what we were like *in* it."

She rubbed the back of her neck. "But that would seem like it would be the same for the orchard, for surely the Martins spend as much time and life in their trees as they do at home—more even. I heard one tale that it was sleep that did it, that while we slept, the heart and soul of us wanders while our body rests, and a bit of us is in every place we sleep regularly in. Another theory in one of the circulars was that there wasn't a difference, at first, but some wizards way back when had trouble with it, and their apprentices thought houses were more difficult, and now we all just *expect* them to be more difficult. One story is that it's those who came before us who linger in the places we live. All I know is it's difficult and then some for me, and every other wizard I've heard tell of."

The lanky wizard shook her head sharply, her braid whipping around in the wind and drawing a large arc through the rivermist that made her and Leyla shiver. "But! You still *do* need all the names of the bricks and slate, hearth and chimney, so we can start there. You're going to focus on all the individual names, so let's review the local brick, and the slate…"

Most of the rest of the walk was planning out how Leyla was going to take the standard stencils for all the usual building materials and adjust the spellscript until she had as perfect a match for everything as she could manage. It wasn't the most difficult task, but it required a lot of precision and a decent amount of understanding of what would cause variations, like the age of the tree when it was felled and the seasoning of it after. She thought Leyla had come far enough in her apprenticeship to do a good job here, but this was going to be her first real task on her own while Hannah wrestled with the more difficult (and intangible) problems, and Hannah *believed* in over-preparation.

As they neared the Milligan house, though, there was an opportunity for a different lesson. "Ah, they must be almost done with Heather Mullen's house; Edith was telling your papa about that. Watch, I always thought this was clever..."

Hannah waved a cheery greeting to the men working on the house, and received some amiable waves in return before they resumed watching their smoke-leaking. A small fire of fresh, green wood was smoking just outside the house, and with a very simple spell rolled out next to it, the smoke was billowing toward the house.

"Oh...I see Mama, they're pushing the smoke at it. And all around it, too."

"Right Ley-ley, and they must have someone inside. Ah, there she is, ayup."

A lithe woman had opened the door and called out an all-clear. "Nicely done, lads! Not a draft in the place, and I couldn't smell a thing!" A bit of a cheer rang out, tinged with no little relief.

"I bet they're relieved, if any of that smoke had made it through both walls *and* the insulation, that'd mean there was something wrong with the brick for sure." Hannah paused, thoughtfully. "Well, or the slate on the roof, I suppose. Not really sure what all they do to keep the roofs all snug, now that I think about it. Have to ask 'em sometime."

Her daughter looked thoughtful. "Maybe the snow is enough to insulate it? Whatever it is must work. I know you and Papa are always saying the new houses are more snug."

Hannah nodded distractedly. "Aye, and they've never asked for a hand on any spellwork there, so it must be simple enough. In any case, I'm right glad of it. We haven't had a truly bad winter since before I had you, but we'll all be grateful when the next one comes. Ah, there's Rae and Tristan now."

The young couple stood in front of their house and welcomed Hannah and Leyla with smiles, though both were muted. Tristan's was easy enough to guess at, as he wrapped a protective arm around his heavily pregnant wife. Rae, though...Hannah wasn't so sure.

"Welcome, welcome! Please, come inside, the wind is brisk today, isn't it? We have some hot soup if you would like!" Tristan bustled about the cosy home, making sure Rae's footstool was at the right distance and providing steaming mugs to everyone. Leyla began happily slurping before a sharp glance from her mother converted her to silently sipping.

"Thank you kindly, Fisher Tristan, it was a mite chilly on the walk over."

"Oh, please, no formality in the house. It's just Tristan."

"Ah, all right...Tristan it is, and in that case I must be Hannah." She wasn't best pleased with that, but it *was* his house...well, his and Rae's. Hannah kept a steady gaze on Rae while her husband continued fluttering, though what it was he kept finding to do she couldn't imagine. The younger woman's eyes met hers easily enough, better than Hannah had been afraid of given how tense things were between Rae and her father. There had been more than one reason for her nerves earlier, and she suspected Ciaran had known that.

"Tris, just settle, love. We'll need to see what the wizard—pardon, wizard*s*—need, won't we?"

Leyla blushed the way she usually did when someone called her a wizard, and Hannah nodded thanks, both for settling down the slightly annoying man and the courtesy.

"Well, the first part will be simple enough. App—ahem, Leyla will take stock of all the physical bits, the brick and wood and suchlike. That might take a few days; we want to be as exact on that as we can. And I'll…" Hannah paused, reaching for the right way to put this to the severe young woman in front of her. "I'll be observing, mostly. Trying to see what makes this a home, rather than just a house, if you know what I mean. I don't know if Foreman Lennox told you, but—"

Hannah paused at the flash of…something, in Rae's eyes. Tristan's tension, not really settled yet, ratcheted up a few notches and he looked over at his wife in concern.

"My…father told us he would be paying for you to try to find the name for our home. If there's anything that will help keep little Sally or Sam from being lost their first winter, we'll take it. We're very grateful." Rae's flat tone belied her words, and Leyla looked at her mother in concern. Even she could pick up that something wasn't right.

Hannah nodded. "Try is the right word. This isn't… I hate to say it, but it's not like most spellwork, where there's a right way to go about it. I'll just have to see what the right thing for here is, if I can. All else fails, though, we can at least make all your usual spells a hair better, but we'll try for a proper name."

Rae gave a curt nod, then winced, causing Tristan to practically leap out of his seat. "What was that? Is it time?"

She waved irritably. "No, it's not time, just a sharp kick. You'll excuse me, all, but the privy waits for no one at this time of it." She rose and walked stiffly out of the room.

Tristan looked apologetically at Hannah and Leyla. "I'm sorry, she's not usually… It's just… I ought to go chop some wood, shouldn't I? Can't have too much of a woodpile!"

After he fled, Hannah whuffed a deep breath of air out, and Leyla cautiously asked, "Wizard Hannah? Is… Does Fisher Rae not get along with her papa?"

Hannah had figured she might have to go through this, though she'd hoped otherwise, and had her answer ready. "It's complicated, Night-star. The year before Fisher Rae was born was one of those awful winters I mentioned. At the time, Lennox wasn't yet the foreman, and the Milligans had been struggling. They only had a half-bin"—Leyla winced at the poverty or carelessness that implied—"and they had one of the older houses. Fisher Rae should have had an older brother and sister…"

Hannah's breath caught, imagining again what she would have done if it had been *her* daughter in that cold.

"They froze. I was just old enough to understand, come spring, and it was the most awful thing that ever happened in my life. Still is, for which I'm grateful, but he… It was like a part of him froze, too. He threw himself into the work at the quarry, made Foreman even though he hadn't been born here. And he made *damn* sure nothing ever happened to his daughter, and that she had everything coin could buy, which isn't nothing."

Leyla's eyes had been wide through all of this, and she opened her mouth when her mother paused, before pausing herself. "A good wizard tries to see what isn't there… Everything *coin could buy* isn't *nothing*, but it's not *everything*, either, is it?"

Hannah's lips twisted, torn between pain and pride. "No, Ley-ley, it's not. And she's made her opinion of him pretty well known because of it. Which hurts him—plenty, if I had to guess. Maybe as much as it hurts her."

She shook her head. "But it doesn't change what we're here to do, and I see you've finished your soup, so let's get to it."

Over the next several days they fell into a steady, if somewhat strained, routine. Each morning, Leyla would catalogue everything she could about the structure, experimenting with tiny variations in the spells to get the best matches possible. Hannah split her time between experimenting with different scripts and watching. At first Tristan and Rae were both stiff about it, but eventually they studiously ignored Hannah as they went about their lives—most of which revolved around fish, sensibly (if smellily) enough, or the tools for handling them. But what really caught Hannah's attention was the *joy*.

It took her a while to understand it. She and Ciaran, and Hannah's own parents, had very different relationships. Tristan fussed constantly, and it wasn't just the incipient baby. Rae hardly had a moment to herself, and was occasionally acerbic about it. But when they were eating together one day Rae was looking fondly at her husband and murmured, half to Hannah and half to herself, "He sees *me*, just me. Spent my whole life stuck behind two ghosts, and now I've got someone who would fall into a ditch before he looked at anything but *me*."

And Hannah could start to see, eventually, how in her (much) quieter way, Rae loved him just as much. There was always another length of line ready before he realised he needed it, and she squeezed his hand just a few moments longer than needed when he helped her out of her seat. And amidst his near-constant burbling of talk, one bit of flotsam stuck with Hannah. "Eight brothers and sisters, you know? Never had a chance of anyone actually *listening* to me, until Rae. She listens to what you say, what you don't say, and what you *meant* to say."

But two weeks in, Hannah was knuckling her forehead. "Yes, I've got insight, I know everything there is to know about the wood and brick and even the *flooded* hinges, but none of it's making sense for the *frosted* name!"

She could hear Leyla give a shocked giggle behind her, and muttered a few more imprecations at herself for swearing where her daughter could hear. "No, I shouldn't have done that, and don't *you* start."

Leyla subsided, and her mother resumed glaring at the different chalked scripts in front of her. "There's something I'm just not... Bah, I'm going to take a walk. Maybe that will clear my head."

"I'm going to stay here, Mama, if that's all right. I had an idea."

"Might as well. Mine seem all dried up."

A good fifteen minutes later, Hannah returned, with windblown hair and red cheeks and no better ideas. But she saw Leyla had erased all the previous ideas—no loss there— and chalked a much bigger script in their place.

"Now, what is this, Apprentice?"

"Well, Wizard Hannah, I thought... Maybe it doesn't have *one* name, exactly, but sort of two?"

Hannah's previous attempts had all been using the simplest and most common format for spellscripts: A central circle, with the scripts modifying the core spell expanding from there in concentric circles. Leyla had switched it to a much more complicated version with *two* circles with their own expanded scripts, which interlocked in the middle.

"I'm… Well done, Apprentice Leyla. That's not an easy thing to pull off. You've even got the middle scripts cohering, well enough for an early draft like this at least. Whatever made you decide—"

She broke off, staring in horror. For a true spell, in the centre of the circles would be the command word or words central to what the spell was designed to do. Simple spells would have one; more complicated ones might have a full circle as their centre. Names, though, had no spell, and the centre was usually left blank, though there might be some nonfunctional script for decorative or personal reasons. And while spellscript wasn't a *language*, exactly, there were ways of transcribing regular words into it.

Leyla had put a word in the middle of each: *Clara* in one, and *Brody* in the other.

Hannah looked frantically around, and breathed partial relief when she saw Rae was down by the river a ways off. *"Who told you those names?"*

Leyla recoiled at her mother's voice. "Pa-Papa did? I… You told me the story, and it was so sad, I just wanted to know the babies' names. And then, I thought, maybe…"

Hannah wanted to pull her hair out. "You *thought* that *maybe* you'd just bring up the worst thing that ever happened to this poor family? You *thought* that…huh."

Leyla stopped flinching quite as much at that "huh." She knew what a "huh" like that meant from her mother.

The wizard had an abstracted look, tracing the lines of the chalked script. "You know…"

She began pulling out stencils, tracing more lines and more still. Leyla tiptoed to the door and took up guard to make sure no one interrupted. Tristan just shrugged when he returned and started working on dinner quietly so as not to disturb Hannah, still tracing hours later. Leyla was worried what he (and his wife) would say when they saw the script, but neither even looked, having given up trying to make sense of the dizzying array of spellwork some days before.

Tristan started to offer a bowl to Hannah, but Leyla wordlessly stopped him, shook her head, and took the bowl. She sat patiently beside her mother, waiting for the right abstracted moment to hold up a crust of bread soaked in soup, or a spoonful of vegetables and fish from the bowl. Hannah chewed and swallowed as if she hadn't the faintest idea what she was eating.

As Rae settled into her favourite chair with a sigh of relief, and Tristan sharpened his knives (and Leyla worriedly looked at the sinking sun), Hannah drew a quick link to the light spell they used for testing, and it lit. She traced another, and another, and in short order three light spells were glowing dimly.

"Hah! That's it, Night-star, you are a genius! I—oh, Fishers Rae and Tristan, ah." Hannah quickly looked around, took in the time and blanched a little, looked back at the name and blanched more before quickly scrubbing out the words in the middle of each, and then collected herself. "I— No, *we* have a name for your home."

Tristan brightened immediately, and came over in excitement. "Oh, how wonderful!"

Rae was more cautious. "And…how much less fuel will the spells need, then?"

Hannah looked over at Leyla, who started sketching out various smaller spells, and after a few tests, which they double-checked each other on, Leyla spoke up. "A little less than half the usual, Fisher Rae."

Rae's eyes widened. "You can't be serious. *Half?*" Her husband's shocked inhale echoed her disbelief.

Hannah nodded solemnly. "Half. That's about right, for a good name."

The couple clasped hands for a moment, and Tristan's voice was shaky. "Thank you. Thank you both. Even in a bad winter, we'll be able to keep all our wards running *so* much easier. I don't..."

Rae's voice was firmer, but a few silent tears streaked her face. "Thank you, Wizard Hannah. And thank you, Apprentice Leyla. And...thank my father, please."

Hannah nodded, understanding the layers there. "I will. He did tell me that he wanted to see it installed, if you would allow it."

Rae's nostrils flared, and she took a moment before responding. "For this... Tell him, for this he can come."

Hannah nodded again. "We'll be back tomorrow to finish the fine detail work on it, and take it down proper so Ciaran can make the plate, but we shouldn't have to intrude anymore. And just in time, too: I smell snow on the wind." She winced. "Which also means we need to hurry. My husband is not going to be best pleased with me getting home this late. Come on, Ley-ley, let's see if we can beat the twilight."

With a few last parting thanks, they took off. Not *running*—it was too long a journey for that and far too cold to risk sweating. But walking briskly, certainly.

"You did well, Apprentice Leyla. Very well. Nearly scared the life out of me for a minute there, but well done anyway."

"Thank you, Wizard Hannah. And...I'm sorry I didn't warn you."

"All's forgiven, we'll just leave those off the plate when your father makes it."

Leyla paused. "Mama? Maybe… We shouldn't have it there, no, but maybe… Maybe we should show that to Foreman Lennox? I think…maybe he'd like to know…that."

Hannah shivered. From the cold, right, definitely the cold.

"Maybe, Ley-ley. I'll talk with your father about it."

"About you both being home *well* after sundown?" Ciaran's deep and disapproving voice came from the door ahead.

Hannah winced. "Aye, that too, yes. But, my loveliest husband, I really *did* need just a little longer—"

Ciaran glared at her hangdog look for a long moment before shaking his head and sighing. "I'm sure you did. We'll discuss *that* later. But for now…"

He closed the door firmly behind them, and picked his shivering daughter up to plunk in front of the fire before wrapping his wife in a strong, warm embrace.

"Welcome home."

Banking the Future

Hannah took the last bite of her still-warm oatmeal, stretched, and stood to put on her cloak. "Well, I was hoping this cold snap would break at some point, but at least we don't have to start early."

Leyla already had her cloak on, and was whirling in little half-circles to make it flare out so she could admire the embroidered stars. Hannah smiled tenderly, her heart aching from the sweetness of it. And it wasn't just because Leyla was adorable (though her mother allowed as how she was, in fact, the *most* adorable), but because of what it meant. A few years ago, they were still making do with clothes much less fine than these, since neither she nor Ciaran were more than indifferent at sewing and they hadn't enough to trade for any others.

Her husband kept telling her that they were coming up in the world, and she knew he was right, but seeing how happy her little Night-star was made it hit *home* in a new way for her. And with them about to finish their last obligation to the village before *winter* began, much less Springsfirst... "Next year'll be even better."

"What was that, Mama?"

"Nothing, Ley-ley, just ruminating a little. How about one last spin before we start?"

Leyla tilted her head, then laughed with glee as her mother swept her up and out the door, laughing and spinning her a full few circles before plunking her down with a kiss on the top of her head. "We should start *every* day like that, Mama!"

Hannah laughed again. "*Every* day seems a bit much, but who knows? On days like this, I think I could be convinced!"

They chatted cheerfully as they walked through the mid-morning sunshine. Hannah felt that she probably *should* go through some history of earth spells or the like, but Leyla knew what she needed for today, and despite the chill in the air it was gorgeous. The purple of the heather, the sheer blue of the sky, and the babble of the river as they approached were like a balm on Hannah's usual restless energy, and both were smiling and laughing still as they made it to the riverbank.

"All right, Ley-ley, you know what to do: Start here and hopscotch me when you're ready for the next one."

Leyla nodded brightly, and undid a small latch before (with a grunt of effort) she pulled the slate cover out of the divot of earth it was inset into, gently setting it aside. She then pulled her stencil out of her pack before setting it against the stone set into raised earth next to the river. She traced it carefully, each line and curve, confirming that the spellscript was fully intact before nodding, pulling the stencil away, and examining every inch for the smallest fracture, the tiniest crack that might warn of a future break in the stone. Satisfied, she put the stencil back against it and checked a second time before following the linkage line to the adjacent bin, and dropping a small bundle of reeds in to its emptiness. Finally, she took a knife from her belt, settled her feet with a look of concentration, and stabbed the riverbank hard with an overhand grip.

The little apprentice staggered a moment as the old knife skittered aside as the ward deflected her strike, but she recovered before she lost her footing. She nodded firmly, put the slate cover back into position to protect the spellscript from weathering (with a few taps from a little hammer to seat it properly), redid the latch, looped the stencil over one shoulder and her pack on the other, gathered up what few reeds the ward hadn't burned, and made her way past her mother to the next stone. Hannah was doing much the same, though moving the slate cover was considerably easier for her.

While not complicated, the work was not easy, either. A great deal of attention to detail was needed, and testing the spell had their arms sore as well as a certain wooziness from being knocked off balance so many times. The worst part, however—and the reason they started so late in the morning—was the cold. The river was low in the end of autumn, as low as it would be outside of winter when the risk of wet snow would make this even more unpleasant, but it still moved vigorously, and the wards were set in areas where the river had rapids, sharp curves, or other areas that would feel more of the force of the water (or anything borne on it). That agitation created spray, and it was impossible to avoid all of it. So by midafternoon, both wizards were beginning to shiver despite their new cloaks, and Hannah eventually had to call a halt.

The next few days were similar, and only the thought of Ciaran's hot stews for dinner in their cosy home made braving the chill again bearable. Hannah and Ciaran both were growing concerned, as this cold had lasted far longer than was normal for the season. But, thankfully, after a week, the cold snap broke, and the warmth made the rest of the work much more bearable (though no less exhausting).

On what Hannah hoped to be the last day of this, Leyla called out to her. "Wizard Hannah? I think there's a problem with this spell, and I think you should come look at it."

"On my way, Apprentice." She looked over the area Leyla was pointing at. "Good catch, Apprentice, that's a small crack indeed. So, tell me, with the size of that crack, and where it is in the script, what do you think the impact to the spell would be?"

Leyla screwed her face up, uncertainty plainly written on it. "Um…I think it would still do what it was supposed to do, but it would *also* activate if a steady wind blew too hard on it, instead of just if a sharp impact hit it? I'm not *confident* in that, though."

Hannah waggled her hand back and forth. "A good guess, and that *might* be what would happen. It might also work as intended, just with a bit less efficiency. No real way to tell without testing it—the crack might be larger or smaller than the surface looks to us. You're right to be uncertain. 'A good wizard is never in so much trouble as when she's *almost* sure,' and all that." She sighed. "And given how much effort it takes to replace one of these, it looks like we'll be testing it. Fl-uster it." She bit her tongue just in time, thankfully, and avoided swearing in front of her daughter. "I'll get the wind spell set up, and while I do that, can you tell me why it's so difficult to replace one of these, Ley-ley?"

"That one I know! It's because they're stone and it takes *so* much work to re-carve stone! With wood, you could just sand it down and re-carve it—well, if it was thick enough wood. Embroidered cloth you can redo the embroidery, metal you could use acid like Papa does—well, most metals—to remove it and then re-etch it, but stone you'd have to carve the whole face off and then re-carve it." She had a satisfied grin on her face, until it shifted into a thoughtful frown. "But, Mama, why *do* we use stone here? Wouldn't something else work better, and be less *risky*?"

Hannah grinned at the disgust in her voice on that "risky," she'd trained Leyla well there…

"Sure, but not as much as you'd think. It's the water that's the problem, mostly. Wood would rot, or fall to pests out here with no one to guard it, and cloth's the same. Metal would rust, at least any metal we could afford to use. Gold would work, sure, but I don't think there's enough gold north of Meldrum for even one of these, and even all the gold in Meldrum wouldn't be enough for *all* of them."

Hannah's lips twisted. "Tried to convince the village council that we'd be better off doing a stone *box* and putting slate *spells* in them, rather than using the slate to protect the stone, but that would have taken four times the stone upfront and they needed the labour for 'other things.' Now we're going to pay well more than four times that in labour for years to come. Well, maybe if this one fails we can convince them to try one my way…"

She finished chalking out a steady wind spell, and pulled out a few chunks of charcoal to power it. After making sure Leyla was ready by the bin and had dropped another bundle of reeds in, and that there was nothing else likely to interfere with (or be interfered with by) the spell, she took a deep breath and chalked closed the activation line.

The wind picked up immediately, as she hadn't bothered with the far more complicated script needed for a gradual increase, and the *uncanniness* of wind pulling away from her but not *on* her was disorientating for a moment, before the regular wind caught up to the spell-wind.

"Always hate that bit... All right, Apprentice Leyla, if the wind was going to trip the ward, it should be doing it any moment. Let me know if it does. Rather save the charcoal, if we can."

"Nothing yet, Wizard Hannah!"

In the end, Hannah let all the charcoal burn down, and thankfully the ward never activated. "Well, I'd say that was a waste of charcoal, 'cept it's much better to burn the charcoal and not need to replace the stone than the other way around."

She sighed. "Have to tell the council about this one though, definitely need to keep a careful eye on it, and we'll want to check it a few times this winter, just in case."

The rest of the tests went as expected, and though both were stiff, weary, sore, and cold, they were *delighted* to be done with the whole thing.

As they trudged their way back home, Hannah reminded herself there was one last thing she needed to do and dragged her bludgeoned thoughts into proper order, making sure she had the right mix of pleased and solemn.

"Well done, Apprentice. Other than the one stone, it was like I had a second full wizard on this one, and I certainly *appreciate* being done with this in half the time as last year. Your father and I have been talking, and we think it's time you earned proper apprentice wages. It's not much to start, but as you get better and better, it'll be more and more. So…"

With appropriate gravity, Hannah pulled a single silver coin from the pouch she'd hidden it in that morning, and with a firm nod placed it in her daughter's open palms. She'd swear it wasn't half as wide as Leyla's eyes, so she figured she must have said it right enough.

"Oh, *Mama*, I…I mean, thank you Wizard Hannah! And I'll thank Spellbinder Ciaran, too, when we get home."

She tried to mimic her mother's nod, but she was so excited it looked more like a bobble than anything else, and it was all Hannah could do to keep the smile from her face.

"You earned it, but I'm sure he'll appreciate the thanks anyway. Now, keep it up, and you'll get another for the Springsfirst festival, though after that it'll probably just be a portion of the meat or fleece or whatever people pay your father with. You know him, though—he'll make sure you get a good bargain for whatever it is."

Leyla nodded. "I wasn't expecting even *one* coin, so that makes sense, Mama. Ooh, I know just what I want to get at the festival! Or should I save it for the big summer fair? Or should I…no, that's silly, I should—"

Hannah risked a little laugh. "Night-star, you are talking to the *wrong* parent about this. If your father didn't handle all that, I'd be a right muddle. But, seeing as we're home now, you should just go ask *him* about it, aye?"

Ciaran was waiting at the door, clearly trying to catch Hannah's eye and see if she had done it, so she gave him a nod and he grinned broadly and braced his back foot. Which was wise, as his daughter ran up and sprinted into his arms, rocking him with the impact.

"Oh, Papa, we found a stone that had a little crack, but it wasn't too bad, and I was so tired and sore but then Mama told me I did such a good job and she gave me a silver coin and I don't know what to do with it but she said I should ask you, and—"

Ciaran grinned, and squeezed his daughter so tightly she stopped talking for a moment with a small "Uck!" before leaning over and kissing Hannah a welcome.

"Well, it seems that the time has come to teach you about *bargaining!* I've been looking forward to this; we can chat over dinner. But, first!"

He closed the door, took their cloaks, and wrapped both of them in a warm hug.

"Welcome home."

Interlude: Winter's Light

Outside the Hendry home, a deep, wet snow had blanketed everything. The muffled silence would have been eerie to those familiar with the land, and during the brief time the sun appeared the overwhelming brightness would have been as disorientating as the silence.

Inside, however, was a different story.

"Ooh, Mama, I think I have one! Instead of using a ward to keep the bugs *off*, I could use one to squish them! It wouldn't use any more power, and it would work just as well, except for how *sticky* the trees would get." Leyla giggled at the ickiness of it. "There would be bug juice *every-where*!"

Hannah laughed out loud at that one, and Ciaran managed a chuckle, though the pained look in his eyes at the idea of that much "ick" was fair enough, given his usual fastidiousness.

"That's a good one, Ley-ley! Let's see, you're at *three*"—she drew another line on the clay they were using to keep track— "alternate methods of protecting from pests, two alternate power sources to keep the wards running without a waterwheel, even if I think a lot of little windmills is a mite silly, and one completely bizarre approach. Not sure how your uncles would feel about using their trees as bait for crickets and such, as tasty as they can be roasted, but I'll admit I'd never have thought of it."

As she ran through the list, Hannah was quite pleased. Despite the silliness, this was good wizard training. Every spell, at its core, was really as simple as could be.

First, you needed some physical representation of the spell itself, whether embroidered or chalked or carved or anything else. You could—and some did—grow flowers into spell patterns. At its heart, the spellscript was really just a way of telling the world what you wanted to do in a way the world would understand. That could be simple or not, but had to be something *doable*. You couldn't magic the sun down at noon, and you couldn't squeeze water out of a clear sky.

Second, you needed a source to power the spell. Many spells, and every spell that did not specify otherwise, was powered by energy from whatever living thing it was touching. But you could use anything that had energy or that could burn (charcoal and coal being common, but burnables of all sorts were used as a pinch). Because of that, anyone could draw (or grow, or anything else) their own spells and power them with all sorts of things, so everyone had everyday spells that worked just fine.

What you needed a *wizard* for was things that either weren't everyday, or when the everyday went wrong, and for that you needed creativity in the why's, the what's, and most importantly the how's of magic. People like Ciaran and Rosie were better at making the stencils or embroidering the actual spells, but they needed wizards to tell them what to carve or stitch in the first place. So using prize cherry trees to lure crickets wasn't likely to be useful, no, but it was for sure and certain something that no one besides a wizard would ever build a spell to do it, and who knew? Maybe one day someone *would* want to use trees to lure bugs.

She grinned at her daughter's beaming (and mischievous) pride, and turned the clay over. "I think that's enough for that one, then, let's try a different idea. Something smaller this time… Here you go, the little spell the loggers use to make sure trees don't fall before they're ready. You know the usual way, they just carve it right into the tree, and it burns a little bark if needed. What other ways can you think of to accomplish the same goal of keeping the loggers from getting squished like one of your bugs?"

Leyla gave a thoughtful "Hm…" as she cleared off the chalk on the cloth she was experimenting on, before heading over to the stencil racks and trading out her ward spells for the (much) smaller tree-steadying spell.

"That ought to hold her for a while, Cirie, might be a good time to go work your metal while she's too lost in thought to ask you a thousand questions."

Her husband started to rise, though a bit hesitantly. "You're sure you want to handle the questions alone? I know it's your first day, and it's always rough for you."

Hannah leaned her head back into her chair, and gestured at her comfortable nest by the fire. "What more would I need? It's a blessing just to be able to *rest* for once. Maybe we'll be able to get enough put by at Springsfirst that I can just take the day each month, but to do that, *someone* needs to have enough stencils to sell."

She grinned up at Ciaran. "Don't worry, I can handle the questions just fine, and if I want you, your daughter will be poking your leg before you know it."

Ciaran laughed at that. "Aye, *that* I don't doubt at all. All right, Hannalan, I'll take the opportunity while I have it." He leaned over to kiss his wife, and gave her a quick squeeze before snagging half a loaf from the last night's baking that comforted their noses with the familiar smell of warm bread, and slipped quietly to his forge.

Hannah enjoyed watching him go before adjusting the hot stone she had on her lap and just closing her eyes for a minute. She knew her daughter would have questions or ideas soon enough, but she didn't need her *eyes* for those, did she?

The days passed cheerfully, for the most part. On occasion, Leyla would get antsy and be sent off to throw snowballs at some of the other village children. On occasion, Hannah would get antsy and be banished by her husband to go collect birch bark or anything else, so long as she wasn't *theorising* at him all the time. And, of course, on occasion Leyla would be sent off on some task or another even when she wasn't being antsy, so her parents could enjoy each other.

Hannah *routinely* blessed whichever brilliant soul in the misty depths of the past had figured out the spells that made children options to be chosen when ready instead of risks to be hazarded on every pleasant evening with a fine man, and it was during one of those blessings that her latest idea came to her.

Ciaran groaned as she sat up a little. "Love, we were having such a nice *relaxing* time, and Leyla won't be back for at least another hour."

Hannah absentmindedly patted him as she reached for the clay she kept beside the bed for just such occasions. "I know, I know, just... I had... Let me just... There, that'll remind me later."

Her attention shifted to fully focus on him as abruptly as it had shifted towards her idea. "See? I'm trying what you said, just making a note. And now, I think it's time for *you* to try *my* idea, so come here..."

The evening ended up being occupied, what with one thing and another, but the next day after breakfast Ciaran went off to convert the last of their household stencils from wood to metal, and Leyla was settled into examining the variations between the same spell for ten different types of rocks to see if she could make more elegant adaptations for the different materials. That left Hannah with the space and concentration to just *focus*.

That tree-steadying spell burned a little bark for power. And that was fine, as the bark of a lot of trees wasn't particularly valuable, not more than anything that burned was in general. For a lot of trees, though, they'd strip the bark from the logs before stacking them, or milling them, or all kinds of other things. That took a lot of time, but it was always worth it for more burnables.

But...what if she could tie that bark-only power source into one of the *other* spells the loggers routinely needed? If it could be efficient enough, they could burn away all the bark, saving the time needed to strip it, and get enough other useful things done to warrant losing burnables. It would save time and use power more efficiently, which was always worthwhile. There had to be *some* reason no one had done that already, but she couldn't think of one right now.

She grinned. And, after all, sometimes the reason no one had done it already was just that no one clever enough had thought of it. Nine times out of ten that *wasn't* the reason, but sometimes…

She started pulling together all her logger spell lore, and began mapping out possibilities. And if her husband or daughter had to nudge her later to eat dinner, what of it? That's what winter was *for,* having time for things. She said as much at dinner after being dragged to the table.

"Well, yes. At least now that we're doing well enough to not have to spin our own thread."

Leyla made a face at that. "Papa's right, winter *without* spinning is nice! *With* spinning, though…ugh. I don't know how people *do* it."

Hannah grinned. "Well, not that I disagree with either of you, but I know Rosie always told me that it wasn't the *spinning* that was fun, it was the singing and storytelling and such that went along with it. Which, aye, I could see being fun on occasion. It's just that none of us here like spending that much time with people, when we can avoid it."

Ciaran shrugged. "There's a reason we took over this house outside the village proper. I like my stars more than I like songs and dances."

Hannah grabbed his hand, fingers circling over the extra-smooth skin on the backs of his fingers in the way she knew he loved, and captured Leyla's too.

"And it's hard to be lonely when I have you two. I feel lucky all the time, you know."

They all smiled at each other for a long moment, before Ciaran's deep voice broke the silence. "I'm very glad! That means you won't mind losing a tickle fight *too* much, then!"

He picked up both Leyla and Hannah despite the laughter and squeals, and nearly made it to the bed before their concerted efforts brought him to his knees.

The rest of the evening was silly, fun, and loving. And as Hannah reflected later, that wasn't a bad way of summing up "happy."

Rough Waters

Leyla's voice was unpleasantly higher-pitched than usual. "But *Mama, why* do we have to go so *early*? The *sun's* not even out yet!"

Hannah gritted her teeth and pushed down the urge to snap at her daughter, though it took some doing. "Because the traders only tracked your father down late yesterday when he was at the market, and we have to get the new spell to your aunt Rosie *today* for her to have enough time to re-embroider their clothes before they head back south. I don't know how long it'll take to figure out the spell they need, so I want every minute we can get."

She raised her hand to cut off Leyla's next whine. "We can sleep in all we want tomorrow, *if* we can do what they need. These are friends of Trader Lukas, and we want to make a good impression. If we can keep getting business like this, it could really *change* things for us, Ley-ley. You might even be able to go study at the *University* some day."

She let more of her hunger for that kind of life leak into her voice than she normally would, hoping it would sink in for her daughter that this was important.

"But *Mama…!*"

Hannah sighed. Well, she'd tried, and she hoped her grandmother's ghost witnessed it. Time for the other approach.

"*Apprentice*, get your cloak on, get your pack on, get your boots on, and *get out that door.*"

Leyla gulped at the taut steel in her mother's voice, and looked down while she finished getting ready. A mulish "Yes, *Wizard*" was muttered just quietly enough that Hannah could pretend she hadn't heard it and focus on stuffing the last of her breakfast in her mouth and getting herself ready. Starting the day with a twanging headache before dawn—not a great recipe for solid spellwork. She took a deep breath as she walked out the door, trying to centre herself, and hoping they hadn't woken Ciaran up.

Their walk to the pier was silent, aside from the occasional stumble in the dark. The sky was thankfully lightening up as they approached, and Hannah just crossed her fingers that Leyla would keep her displeasure to her mother and not make a scene in front of anyone else. At least she'd been able to leave the girl be as they walked… The river traders had tracked Ciaran down yesterday right before he left the market, and said they needed a change to their usual protection spells but had been cagey as to what. Hannah had been mulling it over ever since she and Leyla had gotten back (late, which both annoyed her husband and no doubt was contributing to her daughter's surliness now) from shoring up a few gaps in the frost wards at the Martin orchard, but there wasn't much she could set her mind to without more details.

A whistle caught her attention as they walked out onto the pier that held the trader vessel. "Well, you must be Wizard Hannah! Lukas was always a fair hand at describing folk, and besides I can't imagine why anyone else would be coming here with such a charming girl in tow!"

A rather rakish-looking woman in her late forties with steel-grey hair and a wide grin leapt from the river-vessel to the pier, landing with less of a thunk (and more of a flourish) than Hannah had expected. The chill river mist that was currently seeping into Hannah seemed to be nonexistent to the dashing woman, either, as she withdrew something from her pack without so much as a tremble at the cold.

"And you must be Wizard Leyla! I have a present for you; Lukas said you'd know what to do with it."

The woman bowed, presenting a piece of wood to Leyla, who took it with wide eyes.

"There's fancy writing on both sides... Oh, I see, *Robertson's Blind*, because he kept calling it a hunting blind and—" Leyla broke off with a squeal. "Oh, Mama, on the other side it says *Leyla's Treehouse*!" She clutched it to her, foul mood evaporating in the glow of possessiveness.

Hannah kept her sigh of relief safely internal, and managed a smile that wouldn't set Leyla's temper on edge again. "Well, that's very kind of the good trader! You'll have to thank him properly next time he comes up for his hunting, Ley-ley."

"Oh, I will, I *will*! I know just where to put this! Thank you so much, Trader, Trader...?" She looked up inquisitively.

The woman bowed again, sweeping her hat off in another flourish. "Angelie Palmer's the name, and seeing that excitement was worth hauling that hunk of wood up here all on its own, so I'd call us square." Her grin grew. "'Sides, Lukas paid me to take it, leaving us ahead on the whole bargain which is *exactly* where I like to be."

Hannah grinned a little uncertainly back at that, clearing her throat before asking, "I understand you wanted to change the usual protection spells for your clothing?"

"That I did! But I've heard you're a conscientious type, so I should give you the rundown on the 'why' first, before you think I'm crazy. You ever hear about Bended Fork?"

Hannah waggled her hand. "I know it's a town downriver, that's about it."

Angelie nodded. "That it is, and not just any town. Two different rivers join up there, and the town's gotten mighty rich catering to all the river trade. Rich enough that they got all the farmlands for miles in any direction sending victuals and such to them and listening to the Burgher's Council there. And if that had been that, we wouldn't be talking. They took right good care of us, they did; crew always enjoyed stopping off there."

She scowled. "Unfortunately, the current Council decided that they weren't rich enough, and are tryin' to use all that against us. Food's twice what we used to pay, and drinks three times. Don't even get me *started* on the bedmates and all else! That'd be bad enough, but because they got everybody used to listening to them, we can't even pull up at one of the villages nearby and get supplies, they'll either send us Bended Fork way, or try to charge the same prices. It's a right pickle, and if I wanted brine I'd have sailed the ocean!" She shrugged. "But, now you see why we need you, aye?"

Hannah blinked before speaking cautiously. "I understand why you're not happy with the Bended Fork folks, aye, but I'm not quite seeing what that has to do with the protection spells."

Angelie stared at her, then slapped her forehead. "Ack, I forgot you don't know the riverways! That whole area downriver of Bended Fork is, you might say, *tumultuous*. We get bumped around quite a bit, and our protection spells do their work real well, keeps us from getting bruised and the like."

She grimaced. "A little *too* well. I don't need to tell a wizard how much power that burns, and how much more food we need to eat to make it up. If we tried to run right through, by the time we made it out of the Fork's hinterlands we'd be out of the food we have space for and then some. So what I need *you* to do is make 'em work *less* well. See, if they just keep us from gettin' broken bones and the like, that'll be plenty, we can make the food we can haul last long enough to make it through there, not have to pay those prices, and come out well ahead."

Leyla had stopped being absorbed with her gift some time ago, and chimed in, "But...couldn't you just...take more food with you?"

Angelie shook her head. "Not on those waters. We barely clear them as is. If we took on any more we'd ground out on a sandbar or some of the shallower rocks. Only way to get more food on would be to take cargo *off*, and not only do I have commitments I need to meet and some traders who'd be right unhappy with me for disappointing them, that cuts into my profits! And without those profits, I can't keep the best crew north of the sea, and without a crew then the *Muskrat's Burrow* is *really* done for."

She gestured to the ship behind her. "And I *like* being her captain, so I need another way. I know those protection spells are the best, and when you're close to home or other vittles, it's better not to have everyone sore and healin' and all. And I think my crew would pitch me overboard if I tried to pull this as a *general* rule, but in *this* case, with each of 'em getting some extra coin in their pockets? They'll take some bruises, if that's what it means."

Her habitual grin sharpened. "Besides, once the Bended Fork folks realise we can just skip right past them, and once I spread the word around a bit to the rest of the river-folk, they'll realise they were better off before, aye? Then things'll go back to as they should be, and we can carouse bruise-free."

She clapped her hands together. "Now, that was a lot of jawing, and the day's not getting any younger. Can you do it? Change the spells up so we take a few more bruises, but burn a fair bit less power? And can you get the clothes to us before we have to be on our way?"

Hannah nodded slowly. "We can, aye, both the spells and the clothing, pretty sure. But one last question." She stared steadily into the captain's eyes. "Why not change the spells yourselves? I've dealt with river-folk before—you know the spells of your trade as well as anyone."

Angelie snorted. "Sure, we *might* be able to figure it out ourselves, but we're traders, not *freehanders*. There's a fine line between canny and foolish, and I know which side I aim to stay on!" She shook her head. "No, more than worth it to pay a real wizard to have a look. Mind, I wouldn't normally risk a *hedge* wizard, but Lukas told me about that trick with the charcoal and said you knew your stuff. Said you were the best wizard outside the Guilds in all the Free Rivers, in fact, and he's been up and down enough of 'em that it's no empty praise."

Hannah grinned. The insult and rough language didn't bother her any, not when this captain clearly had the proper respect for how dangerous this could be. Hannah would rather work for someone who needled her from time to time than someone who was *careless*.

She offered her hand. "Done and done then, Captain."

Angelie shook it enthusiastically. "Excellent! You can have these then for reference; a couple of mine are sleeping last night off and won't miss their britches just yet." She handed off a small bundle of clothing, and then whipped her head around. "Charlene! What'n *blazes* are you doing with that? No, don't tell me, I'm coming!"

She clambered back into the boat, tossing a "See you soon, Wizards!" over her shoulder before disappearing.

"Well, Ley-ley, I suppose we better get to it. Your father said Matthew'd let us use the library for spreading out a bit, which'll keep us out of the wind."

And after setting up in the small carefully organised and well-oiled library, the problem quickly became obvious. "That'll do it, Wizard Hannah," Leyla said, "but..."

Hannah sighed, massaging her forehead. "I know, I know. That change'll do exactly what we want the spell to do, but changing that *much* of the spell in that kind of time would tax your Aunt Rosie and every helper she could find. And I wouldn't trust anyone else for *quick* spell-stitching, when we won't have any time to fix mistakes."

She glared at the sun, already heading toward noon. It seemed like only a moment since they'd started working...

"Let's see what else we can figure."

The next few hours were frustrating as they found way after way of changing the spell, successfully, but each one required far too much modification on the existing spell-work.

"Okay, what if instead of changing the entire threshold, we just changed the *amplitude*? It'd still *activate*, but if it wasn't using as much power to blunt the impacts…?"

"Mama, maybe we could just cut the lines between here and here, and have a new little section here?"

"Frost and flood it! That *still* takes twice as many stitches as they could pull off!"

It was a sign of their collective frustration that not only did Hannah not think about the fact that she'd cursed in front of her daughter, but that Leyla didn't even snicker. Hannah started pacing, muttering under her breath, and nearly bumped into the librarian as he came out from polishing the stencils in the back.

"Oop! Sorry there, Hannah. I take it things aren't going too well? Anything I might be able to dig up for you?"

"I don't think so, Matthew." She barked a short laugh. "Not unless you've got a protection spell against breaking that could fit in the palm of my hand, anyway."

"Oh, certainly, just give me one minute."

He slipped away before she could recover from the shock, leaving Hannah and Leyla looking at each other in bewilderment. Even *light* protection spells were a few times that size, normally. What was the librarian playing at?

He returned and with his good hand laid out, indeed, a palm-sized stencil. "Would this work?"

Hannah and Leyla scrambled over to look at it. "Librarian Matthew, that's a *wood* spell! That's not… Unless… wait… Mama?"

The wizard was staring at it. "Sky above and ground below, is it *that* simple? Just trade the script for the wood out for the script for bone? Nothing for the muscle, nothing for the tendon, nothing for *anything*…? The captain *did* say she wanted to draw less power… Not sure she meant *this* much less, though. Well, one way to find out…"

She and Leyla spent a few minutes making the modifications to work on bone, and several more making it as compact as they could manage. It was late afternoon by the time they had a workable spell, and they walked briskly back to the pier.

"Captain! I think I've got something that'll do what you asked for, though it may not be what you want."

Angelie broke off from a small group unloading crates and sauntered over. "You have my attention, Wizard. And what is it that I might not want?"

They quickly explained the spell, and her eyebrows rose.

"Huh. I see what you mean. Well, let's give it a test. Draw it on me and we'll see what happens when Rocky over there wallops me."

Leyla immediately protested, while Hannah…nodded approval. "Aye, little wizard, you're not wrong that it's dangerous, but if it's too dangerous for me then it's too dangerous for my crew. Let's get to it!"

Reluctantly, Leyla steadied the rough stencil they had carved in the library, and Hannah chalked it on.

Angelie called out, "Rocky! I know you're still sore I took you in cards last night! Well, now's your chance to get even, take that pole and see if you can crack my arm!" As an aside, she said more quietly, "Rather have an arm out of commission than a leg or my ribs, just in case."

A large man came striding up with a fending pole grasped in his hands and a wicked grin on his face. "Well, you don't have to tell *me* twice, Captain!" And with more than a little relish, he wound up and smacked Angelie across the left arm.

The pole rebounded, nearly knocking him off balance, and Angelie grabbed her arm cursing and hopping for a minute. Hannah and Leyla held their breath.

Angelie *gingerly* rotated her arm, then reached for the pole and picked it up, hefting it with a wince. "Well, well, well. I'm going to feel *that* for a while, but the arm works. You've got someone who can stitch these for all of us?"

Hannah nodded, breathing again. "Oh, aye, my sister and her people can handle that. I'll get someone to take the design over to her tonight, she'll start first thing in the morning. My husband already arranged it with her, so she's expecting it. She'll get some patches over to you, you can get those on and just take out the activation line on the existing spells, and that should be that. Should even make it easy to switch it back, once Bended Fork comes around."

Angelie laughed, winced, then laughed again. "Argh, aye, I'll be feeling that for a while, oof. And you're right, that *will* be convenient. Now, as far as pay goes, I believe we agreed on—"

Hannah raised a firm hand. "Not with me. I'm a wizard, thank you, not a trader. You can settle up with my husband when it's all done."

Angelie's grin sharpened. "Can't blame a woman for trying. Not that I mind seeing him again—you've got a fine figure of a father there, young wizard, and no mistake."

Leyla blushed a little, and Hannah had a tolerant smile. She *did* have a fine husband, after all. "Then if there's nothing else, Captain Angelie, we'll take our leave. I hope you have smooth sailing, especially under the circumstances."

The captain gave a salute and was about to say something else before a loud crack drew her attention. "Now which flooded fool of you managed to *drop a crate*? I'm going to drop *you* right overboard! Thankee, wizards, and a captain's work never ends!" She loped off down the pier with a wave, and Hannah and Leyla turned to head home.

It wasn't until they were halfway home that Leyla started. "My sign! Oh, no, I must have left it in the library!"

Hannah grabbed her as she started to turn and run back. "Librarian Matthew will take care of it, don't you worry. He's as conscientious as they come, these days. Might have taken losing half his hand to do it, but he's as careful as any wizard. You can pick it up tomorrow. Or—" She broke off, yawning. "Or the next day, maybe. I don't know about you, but I'm *beat*."

Leyla yawned too. "Now you've got *me* doing it, Mama. I just want to eat and go sleep…"

As they trudged up the walk, too tired to even enjoy the fox prints in the snow, Ciaran opened the door and hustled them in. "Come in, come in, I know you must both be exhausted. I've got a nice stew, and then bed for both of you. But, first…"

He gave a steadying hug to both, half-carrying his exhausted wizards.

"Welcome home."

Breathe Free

Leyla giggled as her father made silly faces behind Hannah's shoulder. Hannah didn't even have to look to know that's what he was doing, she would swear she could *hear* his face scrunching. He was clearly in a mood, and she was just glad that tickling wasn't involved.

At a tap on her shoulder, she tilted her head back with a smile for an upside-down kiss with her husband. "Mmm… going to miss this for a bit."

Ciaran grinned back, nuzzling her hair as he returned to arranging baked goodies into their packs. "That *is* the idea of a display like this. I'm up, and *cheerful*, and the sun is barely out! Now you *know* I love you."

Hannah wrapped an arm around his waist. "Well, I had a fair idea you were *fond* of me last night, but you're right, this is *definitely* love. Ley-ley, let this be a lesson to you, look for a partner who'll wake up at odd times for you, much better test than any other I heard of."

Leyla nodded. "That makes sense, Mama, but I like the funny face test too. If they can do good funny faces instead of being serious all the time, they can't be too bad."

Hannah paused and pondered that a moment. "Well, now, you're not wrong there either, Night-star. A good mix of funny and serious, 'cause sometimes you do want serious-ness—that *is* important."

Ciaran's pleased voice came over the table. "We *are* raising her well, aren't we?"

Hannah laughed. "Ciaran Hendry, don't let that smug-gery swell your head too much while we're gone, or you won't fit through the door."

Leyla giggled again as she rose to put her cloak on, trac-ing one of the stars a moment before her father helped her shrug her pack on. Hannah accepted the same service, along with another kiss, before reluctantly heading out. "Don't know how long it'll be, hopefully just the two days, but mines are tricky."

Ciaran's voice followed them down the path. "So long as you don't spend a week optimising everything, dearest. Leyla, I'm counting on you!"

"Got it, Papa!"

Hannah shook her head, knowing there was no use argu-ing. For one thing, she was outvoted. For another…they weren't right, of course, but… Well, they weren't *entirely* right, and…

Ahem. No use in arguing, yep.

It was going to be a fair few hours before they reached Blackhills, but at least it hadn't snowed lately and the trail was clear. Doing this in the snow—or worse, mud—would have been much less pleasant. As it was, they were both grateful they'd had a hot breakfast, but otherwise the day was fine and clear.

"All right, Apprentice, now we're at a good pace we should review the finding spells. Not sure if we'll use those or something else, but I know we've never done much with finding, so it's good practice anyhow."

Leyla nodded. "Ready, Wizard Hannah."

"So: There are two types, generally speaking. You're finding what something is, and you're finding what something isn't. Finding what something *isn't,* you've got the spell searching for every animal bigger than a squirrel that *isn't* a sheep or sheepdog, and you just give it the generalities of size and such, and then the names of what you *don't* want. Not a bad way of finding things that aren't too specific, like looking for wolves or coyotes or bears or anything else that might harry the sheep."

Leyla nodded. "That's a lot like how some wards work, keeps all the bugs and rats and mice and things out, but not the cats or cute little rat terriers."

Hannah nodded back. "Aye, exactly. Findings are a little different because they're usually over a bigger space, oftentimes not too well defined, since mines and fields and such don't stay the same all the time."

The wizard stretched her arms and rolled her neck around. "Ah, there we go. Now, finding what something *is,* that's more likely what we'll be doing today and tomorrow. You send the spell for something specific, with the trade-off that the more specific the more power it has to pull, *unless* you're giving it a very, very good name to work with. Finding all the animals in a field, easy. Finding all the animals about yea high with fleece and no brains? Pretty hard. Finding all the highland sheep with black wool? Darn near impossible…unless you have the specific names of that kind of sheep, in which case it's the easiest."

Leyla nodded slowly. "I can see that, Wizard Hannah. So people must be hard then, as names for people aren't very good."

Hannah breathed out. "Yep. We're too different, too changeable. So, you're down to 'pretty hard' at best, and that means a *lot* of power. That's even before you do whatever you were finding them for, so you can see how these spells burn through your bin right quick."

"Oh, yes. But is there another way to do it? Seems like people would really want to be able to find people."

Hannah grinned. "Aye, that they would. There are a couple of ways. First is hair or the like, something *of* them you can use as a match. Two problems with that, you need a fresh hair on the regular, as the spell gets less efficient pretty much constantly, and the more individual people the spell has to find, the less efficient it gets. People who live in one house? Sure. Everyone who works in a mine? Not so much."

They detoured around a part of the trail that had sunk, pausing for a bit to navigate the rougher terrain of the forest proper.

"Have to tell them about that—be a right pain the next time they bring a wagon down. Anyway, second way is having everyone wear a little script that the spell can find exactly. That's great if everyone is cooperative, and since all the miners are, that's probably what we'll do. Except…" She paused.

Leyla eventually spoke up. "Except what, Wizard Hannah?"

"Except they know all that as well as I do."

Leyla's mouth made an 'O.' "So why do they need us, then? There must be something *else* making it complicated, right?"

Hannah grimaced. "Right. And your father didn't get whatever *that* was from them, so we can't prepare for it."

Leyla winced at that. "And a good wizard would rather be prepared than lucky. But we got lucky with Captain Angelie, didn't we?"

"Aye, that we did, but *she* knew she was asking a lot, and was prepared for it not to work. Not sure the miners are. So, for the rest of the walk I'm going to talk through everything I can think of that mines use, and we'll hope some of it's useful."

The rest of the walk was uneventful, but they could see the loggers had clearly been at work along this stretch of the path, as the forest spread out a bit more. That space allowed them to see sharp ravines with seemingly tiny lakes of breathtaking blue at the bottom, fed by sparkling streams. And in the distance they could see hills: some bare and brown, others rocky, with glinting snow hiding in folds and crags where the sun rarely reached. It was beautiful, in an austere and stark way, and they wondered in hushed tones about how incredible it might look on a clear late summer day when the heather was in bloom and the bees traced their own secret spells across the meandering flowers.

When they made it to Blackhills, the sun was as high as it was going to get on a winter's day, but it hardly felt as though they had walked so long.

The village was, to their eyes, oddly laid out. Part of that was just that they rarely saw other villages, but another part was *this* village existed for only one reason: to support the mine. And sure enough, they could see the mine shafts up on the hills cupping this little valley, easily spotted by the smoke rising from them. A few friendly waves greeted them, returned in kind, as they stopped to rest their feet a minute before making the climb. Everyone seemed to be busy, though, and moved briskly along.

They finally made their way up the northernmost hill ("You could draw your map by it" is what the man had told Ciaran), and were wondering which of the various buildings and shafts to investigate when a raspy "Hallo!" caught their attention.

A burly man stepped out of a building into the sunlight, sneezed a couple of times, and cleared his throat. "Hallo, you must be Wizard Hannah and her apprentice!" His voice was clear now, a clean baritone that made you want to listen to him sing, and he had a broad smile.

Hannah offered her hand. "That we are, and you must be Foreman Brandon. Nice to meet you. Last time I was up this way, Dylan Turnbull was the foreman."

He shook her hand vigorously, and bent down to shake Leyla's as well. "Ah, yes, I took over from Dylan a good two, three years back now. He's enjoying just working his stretch now, and having a bit more time with his little ones." Brandon stood straight, and clapped his hands. "Now, you know why you're here, aye?"

Hannah nodded cautiously. "More or less, something about wanting your filtering spells centralised?"

"That's right. We have to keep the coal and rock dust out of our lungs or we'll end up sounding like geezers before we're forty and dead not long after that. But when we do the usual personal spells they burn hot, on account of the stuff we're mining now. It's coking coal—they use it for ironmongery rather than just straight burning, gets a nice price downriver but it's a fair ways dirtier."

He shrugged. "Keeping us all fed isn't the issue, though. We've got bread and fish and such to spare. But if we don't eat enough greens and such, we start getting queer illnesses. Heard sailors have the like—your teeth start getting weak. We've never let it get farther than that, but we can't get greens enough all year round to keep up with that, and you don't have much've a mine if you don't have miners wanting to work it, so we need another solution."

Hannah nodded. "All right, that makes sense as far as it goes. So you want to centralise it, aye, that's normally easy enough. What did you need *us* for, then?"

Brandon grinned broadly. "We're victims of our own success! Mines are too big for a completely centralised spell, these days—too much efficiency loss. And we're none too sure how to divvy it up without the spells overlapping and burning even *more*."

Leyla replied, "That's where we come in, Foreman Brandon!"

"Right you are! Now, if you want to follow me, I'll get you some gear and show you around." He gestured for them to follow him into a horizontal shaft leading into the hillside, and handed them padded helmets (with some extra padding for Leyla to make it stay), a mask that he tied tightly around the back of their heads ("Sheep bladders—helps keep things out that don't belong"), a shapeless overcoat ("Most of us have our spells on our usual clothing, but we've got these for the carpenters and, I guess, wizards!") and what appeared to be a small nut ("Not that you should be alone, but if you end up alone and get in trouble, crack that open and we'll know where you are and that something's amiss").

They walked through lamplit "drifts," as he called them, which just seemed to be a mineshaft that went sideways rather than down, and he showed them bright yellow markings ("Don't go past these without one of us, means the area beyond might have firedamp or blackdamp, and we don't want you burning up or suffocating, thankee") as well as bright red markings ("Don't go past these—ever. In the red areas is where the circulators pull the firedamp and burn it to help keep our spells going"). They were also shown a large array of miners, including the old foreman Dylan and his wife Sadie, who promised to have them over for a meal if the wizards ended up staying more than a day or two.

After a comprehensive look at it all, which took a good few hours, Hannah and Leyla were both footsore and stuffed with more knowledge than they could use. "Mama, I think we need to eat and think and sleep, maybe not in that order."

Hannah nodded wearily, and Brandon whisked them out, stopping by a green-marked area where the grime that had settled on them was slurped off by an unusual spell on a wiping cloth that Hannah nearly stopped to examine then and there, had Leyla not half-dragged her away. They, presumably, were fed and watered and put out to pasture (or bed, as the case may be), but neither of them remembered much else from that night, being asleep almost immediately.

The next day, though, they were both excited at the problem despite their still-sore feet. "All right, Ley-ley, let's try using different zones and script-finding spells. Everyone in there, even the visitors, has got the same protective spells, so that makes an easy thing to find."

Their first effort was blocked, however, by the verticality. "It's no good, Mama—there's too many people wearing the same things above the mine too, and recognising the difference between 'underground' and 'under a roof' makes it too specific."

Hannah nodded. "Aye, well, if it were easy they wouldn't have brought us. Let's try the idea you had earlier about specific patches that *aren't* the protective spells, and see if that narrows it down enough."

After chalking a script on each of the miners in one of the shafts, they tried again, but were still disappointed. "Well, Mama, that's *better*...but it's still burning awfully fast."

Hannah sighed. "Aye, that it is. I think the spell's having to push through too much earth. Let's see if we can get it to just look *within* the shaft it's in."

That, however, proved too specific once more. They tried several variations, but nothing that used a small enough amount of power to be worthwhile, except for one that *seemed* to work, and had them quite excited, before they discovered that it was only helping the *first* miner it found.

They were dispirited when they stopped for lunch, and ate glumly. The miners on break with them were cheery, however, and amused themselves by playing various pranks on each other to make the two laugh. They were still laughing as they geared up to head back in.

"I'll admit, I wasn't expecting a *rock toad* to come out of her mask!"

Leyla chuckled a little harder. "She got her own back, though! I didn't even know that cats could *do* that, and neither did he!"

Hannah shook her head, hoping that there would not be an epidemic of toad-based pranks when they made it home, but reflected that Leyla was more likely to prank her father than her, so maybe it wouldn't be too bad.

"Let's…you know, that toad gave me an idea. Let's try doing this the *other* way around. Instead of getting the centralised spells to the miners, let's get the spells on the miners to the centralised *bins*. They've got bins spaced pretty regularly for collapse protection anyway."

Leyla frowned. "But…Wizard Hannah, you always say that stretching to find a power source is inefficient."

"Aye, but this whole *thing* is inefficient. And how much efficiency are we going to lose? Two times? Normally that would be terrible, but we were looking at, what, a ten-times loss on our best effort earlier? The whole thing's crazy from a magical perspective, but it's not crazier than trying to feed a whole village's worth of hungry miners greens in midwinter."

Leyla shrugged. "When you put it like that, Mama…"

They found a miner about to go on break, and used him as a test case. After chalking a different version of the filtering spell that would find the nearest bin for its fuel, Hannah walked around with him while Leyla measured the burn rate.

"It's still too fast, Wizard Hannah, I think it's the same problem of going through the earth trying to find the 'nearest' bin."

"Argh. If only there was some physical feature that we could use to guide it… Wait, the cart grooves! All of these have grooves for the carts they use to haul everything, what if we dropped an activation line down all of them?"

Leyla's eyes went wide. "We can't *tie* all the miners to the bins, but that's the next best thing, isn't it?"

"Right! There will still be *some* efficiency loss, but finding an activation line that shouldn't be more than a couple of feet away won't cost *nearly* as much!"

They scrambled back out of the mine to find someone who could cut them long enough cloth strips, and then back in to affix them to a bin. They warned everyone not to trip near the bin as they spooled the cloth out along a shaft, and then chalked an activation line from the bin all the way down the strips, before finding their amiable miner from before and rechalking the spell.

"Hah! That's not even a fifth the loss as before!"

Leyla did a little happy dance, before wincing and stepping more gingerly, and Hannah traded armclasps with the miner before he went back to his work. They gathered up the cloth strips a bit haphazardly, and tracked down the foreman to report their findings. He insisted on seeing it for himself, which Hannah approved of, and then was appropriately enthusiastic.

"Ciaran told me you'd figure something out, and by earth and sky he wasn't wrong! Thank you indeed, Wizard Hannah, and I'll be sure to spread the word that you're a bargain at twice the price! This'll save us no end of grief, and keep the coal flowing. Blackhills thanks you, ladies."

In the event, Blackhills thanked them with a good dinner and hot breakfast (where they had a good chat with Dylan and Sadie and their pack of children), before they started the trek home.

Both Hannah and Leyla were in good spirits, though tired, and the conversation was lively and wide-ranging. "It seems warmer, Mama, I think it might be spring soon! And that means the Springsfirst festival, and I'll have two whole silver coins, and—"

"Could be, Ley-ley, could be. Might be false-spring, though, it'd be a little early for the season to turn, so don't get your hopes *too* far up."

"I won't, but I just *know* it's coming soon! I *have* been doing well, right? I'm earning my second coin?"

Hannah smothered a laugh and nodded gravely. "Yes, you've been doing very well. Just keep it up, and we'll both hope Spring's just around the corner, all right?"

But with all the walking, including on the hard rock in some of the areas of the mine, they were footsore indeed when Ciaran opened the door. He took one look at them, swept their packs off, and picked up Leyla. "I was wondering if I'd see you today. It must have gone well, and you'll tell me all about it tomorrow I'm sure. We'll get those boots off and both of you into bed. But first..."

He set his daughter down in her chair, and went to help Hannah with her boots. She dared to hope a foot massage might be in order as he looked up at her with a sweet smile.

"Welcome home."

Interlude: Springsfirst

Hannah leaned back against Ciaran and grinned. As was often said of the celebration, the music was *almost* as lively as the young folk, and the happy sounds of strings and reed pipes and horns mixed with the laughter and cheers (and aye, occasional tears) of excited people all around.

The council had taken its time on declaring the holiday, worried that another storm might come. Which it did, though with chilling rain rather than snow, and everyone was pleased not to have *that* spoil the day, so it all worked out in any case, despite the grumbling (not least of which from Leyla) at the delay.

"At least the excitement of *being* here finally took her attention."

Ciaran grinned down at his wife. "I will leave aside that you are carrying on a conversation that started inside your head, and just agree that our daughter is much more pleasant to be around now than she was a few days ago."

Hannah rolled her eyes. They'd been married more than long enough for him to know what she was thinking half the time anyway, so what did it matter if she skipped the preamble?

Leyla, for her part, was indeed running around and enjoying herself. After much agonising (and careful nudging from her father during their bargaining lessons), she had decided to only take *one* of her silver coins with her today. She wanted to have a real coin for the big summer fair, and as much as the delayed gratification pained her, she knew full well that it might be a year before she had another coin instead of just barter credit.

Still, though, even one silver was enough to cause a stir among the other children.

"Ley's got a *coin*, how'd *she* get so lucky?"

"Aye? 'Eard she has a little treehouse too."

"Yep, we were clambering all over it before winter—had a grand time!"

"Some kids get *all* the luck!"

Leyla was oscillating between basking in the envy and being proud of herself, and being worried about so many people looking at her and talking about her. One moment she'd be chattering about the adventure to Blackhills (drawing suitable "ooh's" and "ahh's," since few of her age-mates had been more than five miles from the village), the next she'd be hiding behind her Aunt Rosie's skirts or climbing her Uncle Lachlan and perching on his shoulder.

She never ran back to her parents, of course. She wasn't a *scaredy* cat.

Eventually, though, she settled in for serious shopping. Her father had told her not to start too early, before the best things came out; or wait too long, after the stalls and carts would be picked over. There were so many things, though! Lovely fabrics that shimmered and flowed smoothly across wondering fingers, dolls with arms and legs that actually moved and painted clothes, candies made from something sweeter than honey, game boards and elegant little pieces…

"Oh, those dice look so lovely! What are they *carved* out of?"

"Ah, well little lady, these dice were carved from the bones of a great whale! Have you heard of whales? No? Well, they're great fishes that live in the ocean, bigger than ships! Why, some of them are bigger than this entire village, and could swallow everyone here today for breakfast, and still ask for more!"

Leyla shook her head, laughing. That was just *silly*. The trader must think she was *very* little, to believe in fish bigger than a whole village. She danced along, skipping and doing occasional bigger jumps to see things better. She almost passed one cart by entirely, since there were so many grownups in front of it getting papers.

"Must be the cart with all the circulars… But what's *that*?"

Her eye was caught, as there was a beautiful bronze colour that flashed even in the weak sunlight. She jumped, and saw the flash again, but couldn't get a good look at exactly what it was. She frowned, and looked around for the likeliest person to help her get a better height.

"Papa! There's something *flashing* in there, but I can't see what it is. Can you see? Can I sit on your shoulder?"

Ciaran craned his neck over. "Oh-ho, I can indeed. Up you go, Ley-ley, there it is."

Her mouth gaped wide. There were a few playing cards on display, and she could see now that the bronze flash came from a card in the Autumn suit. "Ooh, Papa…look at how detailed the pictures are!"

The cheery woman with the cart finished handing off a few sheets to Thomas Buchan (looking much better than the last time Leyla had seen him, not such a high bar as all that given he had been bleeding out in the charcoal burners camp), and turned to Ciaran and Leyla.

"Ah, Spellbinder Ciaran! I have a few different circulars for you and the missus, some interesting experiments in this one in particular on what different alloys of steel need in terms of protective spells that I think you'll like. And this must be Leyla, then, though I wouldn't have known it with how much she's grown!"

"It's nice to see you again, Trader Holly! And this time, I might be a customer too!"

Holly grinned. "Well, I'm never one to turn down a customer! And if my ears didn't deceive me, I believe I heard you admiring one of these cards."

Leyla nodded, eyes trying to stay on the trader, but slipping back to the cards frequently.

"Well, let me put a few down here where you can see them more easily, let's try one of each suit, hm? Here you are. Now, Spellbinder, there's a new circular I thought you might be interested in, I've got a page here you can read and see if you think it might be worth subscribing…"

Leyla was lost, eyes wide. Trader Holly had put down picture cards from each suit, and the young wizard looked them over in order.

The Spring card was the River, lowest of the picture cards in most games. The River meandered across the card, splashing over the edge, with bright greens and fresh flowers practically unfurling before her.

The Autumn card was the Grove, next up in rank. This was the one that had caught her eye, with bronze trees and leaves of red and orange, yellow and brown, with a few curling away on an unseen wind.

The Summer card was the Field, and this shimmered in golden grain and ripe fruit. Leyla didn't even *recognise* half the fruit, and she spent what seemed like an hour trying to find every different type there was on the little rectangle.

And last, but certainly not least, were the Stars of Winter. This card depicted one of the winter constellations, the Dancers, shown this time as a pair of older women with the location of each star being another jewel adorning their elaborate, if not entirely chaste, outfits.

"Well then, young wizard, what do you think?"

Leyla jumped, startled out of her reverie, and belatedly remembered one of her father's lessons. "Oh, well, they're *pretty* nice, but I don't know, there's a *lot* of nice things today..."

Holly's lips quirked as she tried not to laugh at the air of attempted nonchalance on the child's face. "Well, that's certainly the truth, I can't deny that, can I, Spellbinder?"

Ciaran just shook his head, rubbing the smile off his lips. Clearly, this was one area he'd have to work on a little more with his daughter...

"But, needs must and all, and I certainly don't want to miss a potential sale. Tell you what, seeing as the Hendrys have always been good customers, I think I could cut you a discount and let you have it for...well, I'd hardly make anything, but three silver and a few metal stencils for the deck?"

Leyla's face fell, and she looked at her father. Ciaran cleared his throat and raised his eyebrows significantly.

"Oh! Right, um, Trader Holly, what do you take me for, a…a banker in Meldrum?"

Her father nodded encouragement.

"I suppose they might be worth that if they were made with real bronze! I s'pose I could take them off your hands, though, for…" She groped wildly for a sum, before ending hesitantly, "…half a silver?"

Holly threw her hands in the air extravagantly. "What, did I offend your mother somehow? Have I cursed you and your kin, such that you would wish to curse me to destitution? I don't want a wizard's curse, though, so I'll let you have them for two silver, flat."

Excited at her success, Leyla bounced as she replied. "Destitution! I think you'd be cackling like a fox at two silvers! I couldn't *possibly* go higher than, than…three quarters a silver, and I re-carve the protection spells on your axle!" She added apologetically, "They *are* looking a little faded, Trader Holly. That's not part of the bargaining, Wizard Hannah wouldn't be happy with me if I saw that and didn't mention it."

Holly made an odd noise that sounded a little like "snrk!" and looked helplessly at Ciaran, who had to turn away to keep from cracking. Sometimes she was just *too precious*…

"Well, thank you kindly then, and I understand. We can get back to the bargaining then, Apprentice Leyla."

Leyla nodded, took a deep breath, and repeated, "Three quarters a silver, and the protection spell!"

"Bah, do you think this is my first time up the river? I couldn't possibly do it for less than a silver, the protection spell, and two stencils! And that's my final offer!"

Leyla opened her mouth, paused, then opened her mouth again. "I'm sorry, Trader Holly, this is my first time trying a *real* bargain. Is that *actually* your final offer?"

Holly nodded apologetically. "Yes, it is, thank you for asking. And, might I say, you did an *excellent* job! Of course, you *do* have a good teacher."

She winked at Ciaran, who'd manage to turn around with an appropriately grave face by this point. Leyla looked grim. "Thank you, Trader Holly. But...I have the silver, and I can re-carve the axle before the fair ends, but..."

Ciaran cleared his throat. "Apprentice Leyla, I could use some help with my forging. Your schedule's irregular, but let's say...fifteen hours, I think that would be worth two *simple* stencils for the good trader."

He raised an eyebrow at Holly, who grinned back. "Oh, aye, simple enough...for an experienced Spellbinder like yourself."

Ciaran laughed and waved, conceding the point. "Fair enough. So, what do you say, Apprentice? Fifteen hours' worth of help with my forging? It'll mean less time in your treehouse."

Leyla pondered. Fifteen hours was a long time... Her eyes snuck back over to the cards.

Not as long as she would enjoy *those,* though.

"Yes, Spellbinder Ciaran. And Trader Holly, you have a deal!"

She raised her hand up, and Holly shook it firmly. The trader then started to pack up the cards, before Leyla spoke up.

"Not yet, please, Trader Holly. Can you give me your stencil for the axle, first? I'd like to do that before I take the cards."

Holly paused, then nodded and rummaged a moment before she handed over a flexible leather stencil. As Leyla plonked down and got to work with her knife, Holly murmured to Ciaran, "Not many kids that conscientious. Nicely done, Spellbinder, nicely done. Makes me regret not tripping you into a hay bale even more than I already did."

Ciaran's murmur was equally low. "Now, Holly, you know I wouldn't do well on the move like that, and I'd worry myself sick with someone gone a season at a time. Besides, I know for a fact that you still find your fair share to trip, and don't have to worry about who catches your fancy next visit, so don't try to tell me you are still *pining*."

Holly laughed, and tied up the cards with a little ribbon. "Well, you're not wrong at that! Give my regards to Hannah then, Spellbinder, and let me know what you two decide on that new circular."

Later, when Hannah, Ciaran, and Leyla were finishing their yellow cheeses and dried fruits (the yellow cheese symbolising the sun returning to being up for more than half the day, and the dried fruits symbolising the need to use up the last of the winter stores), they all traded stories of the day.

"Well, since we already turned in our various obligations to the village, I didn't have to wait in the blasted line to register the family for the year, so *I* had a very nice time catching up with Lachlan and Calvin. Little Anabelle is getting almost to the point where she'll be interesting instead of a lump, too."

Ciaran reacted in mock horror. "Hannahlan, is that any way to talk about your own niece?"

"It is, I'll be a much better aunt when she can carry on a conversation, I promise. Until then, taking care of my own lump was enough."

"Hey! I wasn't a *lump*! I was *adorable*."

"Listen, just because you were *my* lump and *I* thought you were adorable, doesn't mean you weren't a lump. *I* used to be a lump, it's just how folks are until their brains grow in."

The conversation derailed a moment as Leyla endeavoured to prove her non-lumpy status, while Ciaran serenely refereed. Eventually, Hannah conceded the tickle fight with a laugh.

"All right, all right, no more calling people lumps, you win!"

"Good! My own *mama*, calling me a *lump...*"

"And how about you, Cirie? Holly Baxter tell you that she should have taken you when she had the chance again?"

Ciaran rolled his eyes. "She was lovely as always, and was a good sport about bargaining with Leyla. I don't know why you always ask that."

Hannah raised an eyebrow. "Did she, or didn't she?"

Ciaran smirked a little. "Well..."

His wife grinned back. "Thought so. Just remember how many different, *inventive* ways I have of dealing with little river trollops and those who run off with them."

Leyla tilted her head. "What's a trollop?"

"A, ah, type of frog, Ley-ley."

"Oh, okay."

Ciaran pulled his wife in for a kiss. "No trollops for me, thank you." And, more quietly, he added, "Nice save, too. Until she decides to go trollop-hunting in the river with her friends."

Hannah sighed. "Look, if that's the worst she gets up to, I'll call it a parenting win."

The last performance rose to a loud crescendo, and the dancers twirled and leapt with it before hitting one last note and pose, and the crowd hooted and clapped, the Hendries included. And with that, the festival was officially finished.

"What a good day, Mama, Papa!"

"That it was, Ley-ley, that it was. Come on, Night-star, time to head home. And hey, for once, it might be *us* welcoming your *father* home! Last one there's a rotten egg!"

Hannah took off at a jog, with her daughter close behind. Ciaran just walked, a wide smile on his face. After all, it might be nice to have them welcome him, for a change.

Ploughs Shared

Hannah was absentmindedly eating her oatmeal (unsweetened today as she knew she wouldn't even notice) while sorting stencils into various sections of her pack. Speed was going to be key, and they were going to have a *lot* of stencils to sort through. If all the animals in the area weren't already being pressed into use, she'd have seen about borrowing a pony, but that was just wishful thinking in planting season.

"Mama, I have all of the barley stencils in my pack, except for one, do you have it over in your stack?"

Hannah blinked, and poked through the rest of the ones she hadn't sorted yet. "Ah, yep, here you go Ley-ley."

"Thanks Mama! I'm hanging the kale and rye ones over here. I know we shouldn't need them for a bit but I figured if someone had questions, it would be easier to find them for the next day, then."

Hannah gave a warm smile, only partly hindered by the mouthful of oatmeal she had just taken. Her daughter really had gotten better at thinking *ahead*, and that was no small blessing. She swallowed before replying with "Good thinking! Probably won't happen, but won't hurt us to have those better organised anyway, and will help in a month or two, for the kale at least, if nothing else."

She finished placing the stencils for the oats, broad beans, and land names, and suppressed a groan as she lifted the pack. What she wouldn't give for a pony for the next month…not least of which because she was none too sure Leyla could handle the weight.

"Your pack not too heavy, Apprentice? We don't want you tuckering out before the evening."

"I've got it, Wizard Hannah! I've been practising carrying things up to the treehouse, this won't be too bad."

Hannah bit her tongue before she asked again, knowing that would only draw a less cheerful response. Last year she'd had Ciaran helping her carry everything, but that had been a waste both because it wasn't *that* much more than she could manage and because there was a lot he could do with that time, otherwise. If her daughter could manage this, they'd be able to earn half again what they had last year during planting season…

If.

"All right then, let's get to it!"

The first stretch of their journey was short, far too short to be worth any lessons. And indeed, this job was one of the few things they did that they knew entirely what they were going to do and how they were going to do it. Well, Hannah did, anyway, and Leyla would pick up on it easily enough. The only real question was how *fast* they could do it.

"Hallo, Farmer Zachary!"

A stout man of middle years was already hard at work on the first ploughing of the little strip of land on the lee side of the hill. The two oxen from the village moved steadily as they dragged the heavy iron plough (also on loan from the village) through the rye that had been growing there as a cover crop all winter.

"Hallo, Wizard Hannah, 'Prentice Leyla. Sky willing that windmill my niece fixed up will *work* this time, so the spells should be up there, thankee kindly."

"Right! Switching from rye to barley, aye?"

"That I am, that I am."

"Then we'll get out of your hair!"

She started striding up the hill to the somewhat rickety-looking windmill at the top, and let her pack slide to the floor with a sigh of relief. She saw Leyla do the same, and tried to keep an eye out to see *how* tired she might be.

"Okay, Apprentice, start taking down those rye spells while I sort out the barley. And if you have questions, now's as good a time as any, not like I have to think much on these."

Leyla nodded and got to work. "I *did* have a couple, thank you Wizard Hannah."

The young apprentice started by carefully unhitching the axle that connected the windmill itself to the power stone, which would ensure no accidents from any half-removed spells. Next she started removing the slate covers from the stone, and pulling the planks of wood that had the ward spells for the rye carved into them out from under the slates. She then started smoothing the spell out of the wood before speaking again.

"Why *is* it that we don't just keep the rye spells aside and put them back on come late autumn? Seems a waste to keep smoothing out the wood and recutting each time, and we don't do it that way for the Martins' orchard, they just have the same spells all the time."

Hannah let her hands and eyes focus on rearranging the usual stencils around the base name for this strip of field, starting to chalk her first attempt onto the stone. "A few reasons, Apprentice. First, the name's a bit different depending on what has been happening with the crops and the land. That doesn't matter as much for the Martins as they just have the one type of tree, but I'll be checking in on that and adjusting the names there too, from time to time. But for this type of farming, the land after a barley crop last year is different than the land after a broad bean crop last year, so even though the *rye* is the same, the *land* isn't, so we need to adjust the name."

Her first attempt was drawing too much power, so she wiped out the chalk and started a second. "Second, each farmer's got a different idea of what they want their wards to focus on, and which farmer works which strip of land changes, based on how many hands they have, how much other work they're doing, all that kind of thing. The Martins aren't going to change their focus too quickly, if at all, but Farmer Zachary's much more worried about pests than he is about frost or wind, where another farmer might think he's got a way to handle weeds and want more wind wards."

This attempt didn't draw too much power, so she nodded satisfaction and took over the first smoothed plank from her daughter to start carving the new spell.

"Plus, it depends a lot on what kind of power is running the wards. Until this windmill started working again, they were using ox power for the wards around here, and that was both a lot less regular and more expensive. The wind blows near constantly, at least right here, so you can depend on it a lot more than oxen who are going to get pulled for all kinds of work around the village."

Hannah blew the wood dust off, checked her carving twice, and then placed it on the stone before starting on the next. "All in all, there's just too many variables. Maybe if everyone had a powerful watermill like the Martins, the difference in efficiency wouldn't matter that much, but that takes an awful lot of coin. We're getting there—more wind-mills and watermills, and better ones too, are coming up every year, but for now efficiency in power's the name of the game."

Leyla nodded slowly. "I can see that, thank you. One more question for right now, then: *Why* is Farmer Zachary ploughing the rye under? Shouldn't he be harvesting it, so we can eat it? Or at least use it as animal feed?"

Hannah grinned, knowing how her daughter would react to *this* answer. "Well, it's because he isn't full of manure."

Leyla narrowed her eyes, glancing up suspiciously at her mother. "I can't tell if you're joking or not, Mama."

The wizard laughed, setting the next plank into place. "It's just the truth! If he had manure enough for all his fields, he'd use that instead, but he didn't quite get hold of enough for all his fields this year, and this one didn't make the cut. The fields need more life in them to keep growing, and one way to do that is to plough the rye under, so that's what he's done."

Hannah wrinkled her nose at the dust, nearly sneezing before setting the next plank in place. "Mind, I think this is the *only* field he's doing that on, between his cattle and pigs and all the sheep around there's enough for all the rest, but I say it again: He's doing it because he isn't full of manure!"

She couldn't help laughing that time, and Leyla's giggle joined in. Thankfully, the last plank was now done, and they could replace the axle and do a final test of the wards. After they both nodded approval there, they replaced the slates that protected the wood from the elements, and headed out to the next farm, waving a goodbye to Zachary Donald as they left.

The rest of the day was much the same, though the crops differed. Broad beans, oats, and barley made up the most, with occasional other crops (with the farmers for those providing the stencils) sprinkled in for good measure. They spent a lot of time in windmills, watermills, ox mills, and even one farm where the family had decided to use burnables for their wards. Hannah privately thought they were fooling themselves, and that strip was going to cost them more than it was worth, but she had already tried to dissuade them and it was their experiment to make.

All of this was pretty routine, except for Hannah keeping a careful eye on her daughter. She was asking a lot of Leyla, and she guessed Leyla would fall flat on her face before admitting she was tired. At least most of the time they could do their actual spellwork while sitting, and the different strips of farmland weren't terribly far away from each other, so they could frequently rest their legs.

"Here, Night-star, let me take that pack. We just have one more for today, and I can handle both packs now."

She knew she'd guessed correctly when Leyla just nodded, rather than protesting. Hannah's back wanted to protest, but that was what husband back-rubs were for, later.

Their last stop for the day was a bit unusual: a new apple orchard where the saplings had finally grown enough that Heather Mullen was ready to have her pigs graze there to keep the weeds down, so she wanted the wards refocused on other types of pests. Hannah handled almost all of this one herself, as Leyla was stumbling as she pulled off the protective slates, and to keep her awake Hannah sent her to go make friends with the pigs.

But finally, it was done, and they were trudging their way back, Leyla half-asleep on her feet. Hannah had trouble relaxing into her backrub later, worried about what the next day would bring.

And, indeed, Leyla *was* tired. But she also had the resilience of well-fed and well-cared-for children in most places, and was ready to show she was up to it. "No, Mama, I can do it! I'm an apprentice now, not a little kid, and I want to prove it!"

Hannah twisted her hair around a finger, since Ciaran wasn't there to chide her, and reluctantly agreed that as long as Leyla could keep going, they really *needed* her to. Ciaran had his own commitments now, and though people would understand if he had to back out of them, that would make it harder to get *him* the kind of work he wanted, if people weren't sure they could rely on him.

"All right, Ley-ley, all right. But we're going to alternate: I'll carry your pack every third walk, okay? I'd rather have you less tired at the end of the day."

And over the next few days, they managed. Barely, but the line between almost succeeding and almost failing is an important one, for how thin it is. And after the first week, Leyla started doing better, enough that she regained her usual curiosity.

"Wizard Hannah, what was that odd cart Farmer Joseph had the team pulling? It didn't look like a plough, and I thought he was done ploughing anyway?"

Hannah smiled. She was so happy that her daughter was back to questions, she didn't care how many were pelted at her, at least for now. "That is a seed drill, Apprentice Leyla. I've read about them in some of your father's circulars, they've been using them *way* downriver, and they are supposed to mean you can use a *lot* less seed in your sowing. I don't fully understand how, mind, but you could ask your father and I'm sure he'd go through the circulars with you."

"It seems like an *awful* lot of metal..."

"Aye, that it is. There was quite the fuss in the village council when the farmers brought it up, and eventually they decided the village would buy one and experiment with it. Farmer Joseph was against it, but he's an honest man and one of the most experienced farmers we have, so they decided he'd give it the first try. He's using it for all his fields this year, and seeing how it does on the different crops. Cost quite a bit of hard coin, but if it really saves as much seed as it's supposed to, it'll be worth it."

"Ohh... That's why we're doing something different with these wards, then. He's sowing the seeds differently, so he's worried about different things going wrong."

Hannah nodded as Leyla thought it through.

"No *wonder* it's worth it to have us come and do all the wards every year!"

Hannah grinned. "Well, that and just the usual labour shortages, come planting. Not *everyone* in the village is part of it—Shepherd Finlay's got better things to do—but most everyone is. They probably *could* manage this on their own, but it would take them a lot longer, not being as familiar with the names and spellwork, and they just don't have the time to spare. Having us do it is faster, surer, and means they can focus."

Leyla nodded back. "I see, thank you Wizard Hannah. It's not as simple as I used to think, farming."

Hannah winced, stretching out her aching back as she put the last plank into place. "Oof. No, not much is. Everyone has been doing this for a long time, them and their people, and if there's even a slightly better way of doing things they're going to try it. There's more to learn about the different kinds of soil than you could learn in a lifetime, at least with the kind of detail the farmers go into with each other, and they're just as much experts in *that* as we are with spellwork."

They began trudging home, Leyla leaning forward to balance her pack. "Well, I'm just glad *I* don't have to do it, Mama. I like being a wizard a lot better!"

Her mother laughed, reaching over to pull her into an awkward, but heartfelt, hug. "I'm glad, Ley-ley, it sure is nice having you with me."

Leyla didn't reply for a moment, and Hannah could feel...*something* about the pause.

"You really mean that, Mama? And not just because I'm helpful? And I am helpful, right? I'm really trying to be, even when I get really tired, but not *just* because of that, right?"

Hannah felt her heart squeeze a moment, and took a breath to carefully reply. "I really do mean it, Night-star. Having my own sweet daughter with me every day is one of my favourite things in the whole wide world. And yes, another pair of hands, and legs on days like this, sure does make my life easier, but I don't just *love* you, I *like* you too. Even *if* you weren't helpful, and you are."

She paused in the road, dropping to one knee without letting any of her aches show in her voice and face as she stared into her daughter's eyes, willing her to understand. "I know I get distracted with things, trying to figure out the next bit of theorising or whatever, but I don't want you *ever* to think that having you in my life isn't the greatest joy I have. I carried you around under my heart for a good while, and just because you're walking on your own two legs doesn't mean I don't still feel the same way."

Leyla's eyes were bright, and she nodded rapidly before burying herself in her mother's shoulder. "I know, Mama, I know. I love and *like* you a lot, too. It's…it's just been a long couple of weeks, and I saw all the farmer kids with their big families, and…thought maybe after you had *me* I was too much work and you didn't *want* another baby because of me, somehow…"

"So *that's* where all this is coming from? No, sweetest, no. The reason you don't have any little sisters or brothers isn't anything to do with you, it's to do with me."

"…Really?"

"Really. You were on the tiny end when you were born, and it…nearly didn't go all that well, for me. Midwife said that if you'd been any bigger, it would have been even worse. Odds were good the next one *would* be bigger, so your father and I decided to stop, then and there."

She hugged Leyla fiercely. "And *you* must have been a blessing straight from earth and water, being the right size for me and all. Couldn't have gotten a better daughter, and if I *could* guarantee a little sister or brother like you, I'd do it in a heartbeat."

Her voice was shaky. "So no, nothing to do with you. And your father and I *love* you, and we're so happy to have you. All right? Any other deep hurts you're just carrying around putting a brave face over?"

Leyla shook her head, still buried in her mother's shoulder.

"Good. Then one last squish—"

Leyla squeezed as hard as she could, and Hannah's arms were just as tight.

"And let's get home before your father wonders what happened to us, hm?"

"Okay, Mama. And…thank you. For telling me."

"What're mamas for?"

They walked the rest of the way back in silence, but Leyla's little hand snuck into her mother's and stayed there the whole way.

"Ah, there you two are! Hannah, what on earth did you do to your knee, did you just stop and kneel in the mud somewhere?"

Ciaran's voice was more confused than horrified, but he stopped at the look on his wife's face.

"Aye, I did, but some things are worth muddy knees."

Leyla hid her face behind her mother's cloak for a moment, before taking her outer clothes off and getting ready for dinner. Ciaran nodded slowly, knowing he'd get an explanation at some point.

"Well, mud's easy enough to deal with, not to worry. In any case—"

He squeezed his wife's and daughter's hands, not knowing why, but knowing they needed it.

"Welcome home."

Tempered Fire

Hannah fussed with the ties of her cloak, again, trying to get them to hang straight. Her lunch was half-eaten in front of her, and Leyla was looking up at her with a puzzled expression.

"It was pretty straight *before*, Mama…"

Ciaran's hands gently moved his wife's fingers away from the ties, and made a neat knot. "There, love. Now finish your lunch before you forget, *again*." He planted a gentle kiss on the top of her head, briefly massaging her shoulders.

"I know, I know, I just…a *University* mage. You *know* how tongue-tied I get, sometimes, and I just *know* this is going to be one of those times…"

Her husband pulled lightly on her braid, tilting her head back at him. "Hannah Hendry, I do not recall giving you leave to worry yourself to death. Now *eat*, unless you'd rather I feed you."

His tone was only half-joking, and she sighed, scooping up the last of the oatmeal and dried fruit. Leyla, having finished earlier, came over and patted her shoulder. "It'll be okay, Mama. She'll see how smart you are and you'll start talking about alternate rune patterns and kaleidosoapic effects—"

"Kaleido*scopic* effects."

"Right, those ones, and she'll see what a good wizard you are and everything will be fine except that Chiefsmith Quinn and I won't have any idea what you're saying, and *that's* nothing new."

Hannah gave a wan smile. "I hope you're right, Ley-ley. I hope you're right."

Ciaran dropped a purse next to her. "She might be, for all you know, never having *met* the woman. And besides, just remember that we are *paying* her. This is not some favour she is doing us. And since she is willing to take work like this, she can't have been terribly well-regarded, despite passing her exams."

Hannah's lips quirked. "Weren't you the one telling me the other week that it's the people at the bottom rung that object the most to someone else climbing the ladder?"

Ciaran shrugged, conceding the point. "True enough, but what good is worrying about it now going to do for you?"

She pushed herself to her feet, heading for the door. "Not a thing, aye. Come on, Apprentice, let's go learn how to enchant an anvil."

And with that, the pair strode out. For once this season, neither carried an onerously heavy pack, and while the weather couldn't quite make up its mind whether to be sunny or showery, that alone made them feel happier about the trek.

"All right, Apprentice Leyla, to keep my mind off things as much as anything else, let's review: What, *specifically*, are we trying to learn about this spell? Or spells, I suppose it could be."

"We're trying to learn how to make the magic *controllable* by the smith, Wizard Hannah. We know how to move heat, and keep heat, but not how to change how *much* heat the spells do, not the way Chiefsmith Quinn does on her current anvil."

"That's right. But seeing what's different is easier if we know what's the same, so let's run through the usual spells for moving and keeping heat."

Leyla opened her mouth to object, as they'd done that last night, and the day before that, and then looked at her mother twisting her hair. "Yes, Wizard Hannah."

Thankfully, for both of them, the walk to the black-smithy wasn't very long.

"Wizard Hannah, Apprentice Leyla, welcome! You're a tad early, though that's no bother, we'll just be finishing this up for a moment."

Hannah nodded, and Leyla hopped up on a bench, curious to watch. The grey-haired blacksmith focused back on the anvil, long hands tapping her small hammer twice on a glowing bit of iron. Her striker adjusted his aim, and struck at exactly the angle she had indicated with a much larger two-handed hammer. The smith then tapped three times on a different section, and a second striker hit that place notice-ably harder. This continued for a time with the two strikers alternating, until Quinn nodded and they moved the piece, still glowing the same colour, off the anvil.

Shortly after it left the anvil, however, the colour began changing, and Hannah nodded as she watched the strikers manoeuvre it. "See that, Ley-ley? The anvil's enchantment keeps it at the right temperature the whole time, so's they don't have to keep moving it from the forge and back, but the moment it leaves it starts cooling."

A voice called out from behind them. "*Technically*, it begins cooling once it leaves the space defined by the spell array. It wouldn't *do* to have it begin losing heat every time they turned it over, would it?"

Hannah flushed, and turned slowly, gesturing sharply at Leyla to come join her. "Greetings—you must be Mage Caitlin."

"And you must be Hedge Wizard Hannah. And…apprentice, I presume. Leya, was it?"

"Leyla, Mage Caitlin, and it's an honour to meet you!"

"Yes, I imagine it is. Now, I take it you have my payment?"

Hannah nodded, handing over the purse Ciaran had given her earlier. The mage opened it and counted out the coins. "It's not that I don't *trust* you, of course, but I do prefer *certainty*."

Now Leyla's face was flushed, and only Hannah's nails digging into her hand kept her from an outburst. "Aye, that I can understand. A good wizard never trusts what she can verify, and all."

The elegantly dressed woman replaced the coins and tied the purse to her belt. The smith's face, blank until this point, tightened as she realised the mage was not going to offer to return the purse. Hannah would have refused, of course, but it would still have been *courteous*.

"Well, now for the demonstration. You have the new anvil ready, Wagesmith Quinn?"

The smith's face was stony as she gestured, and the three wizards followed her around the side. The mage carefully inspected the clearly new anvil, imperiously gesturing for Hannah to come over while she pointed out various features that would be important to the enchantment. Leyla understood less than half the words they were using, so she just stayed by the smith, who had crossed her formidable arms as she watched the interplay.

"She's not as nasty while talking her actual trade, thank the fires." Quinn's voice was pitched just for Leyla's ears.

"Not *as* nasty… But still nasty." The young apprentice's voice followed suit, though considerably higher than the smith's.

"Does good work, though. Never had a one of her spells fail, and more efficient than most of the University types. Makes it worth putting up with her manners."

The blacksmith's voice turned dry. "Barely. But come, not much we can do here, and I wanted to have you take a look at one of the house wards. It hasn't failed, yet, but the spell could do with some renewing."

"Of course, Chiefsmith Quinn, I'd be happy to." Leyla turned and followed Quinn toward the house proper, leaving Hannah and Caitlin to their work. And *work* it was.

"So, with all the variables properly identified, we can now begin constructing a spell matrix with the necessary customisation. We will, of course, start with Ommadon's foundational web, followed by the hexagonal version of the Carolinus Constant."

The mage sighed. "I suppose I'll need to explain all of those to you."

Hannah gritted her teeth before replying. "No, that's all right, I've read enough in my circulars to follow you so far."

Caitlin's eyebrows rose. "Really? Well, who'd have thought, a hedge wizard who can read. In that case, let us begin. I have the stencils here, you may begin chalking them out for the first part of the test."

Hannah unclenched her firsts, and began sketching out the spell. It took some time, but thankfully Caitlin refrained from further acerbic comments while she took out a wildly different stencil, in a bizarre (to Hannah, at least) triangular pattern, and began filling in the hexagons Hannah had drawn inside the outermost circle of the spell. Once Hannah had finished, the mage held up a finger to stop further questions until she finished drawing.

"There! Now, you can see the Solarian triangles—"

"Close off different sections of the hex, aye, I see that right enough. But *how* are they doing everything the spell is doing? I can read the spell right enough, but nothing in the script lets the smith set the different temperature thresholds, and I know it has to be doing that somehow."

Caitlin smirked. "Because you aren't reading all the spells. Start here—" the mage pointed an imperious finger "and continue to there, as if this were an independent spell, not a spellgram."

Hannah suppressed her frustration and read as instructed. Then her eyes widened.

"That's a complete spell. They're all complete spells in *addition* to being components of the whole? You get twice the information density, oh, I can see why that's important on an anvil, such limited space, but…!"

"Precisely. As I'm sure you can imagine, designing a spell that worked as a whole and with each possible combination independently was quite a triumph. Acclaimed as a masterwork among masterworks, and indeed allowed the researcher who developed it to retire once she sold the results to the various guilds."

Hannah rocked back on her heels. "I can see why. I can also see why we don't do this often, though."

"Quite. Several years of research and experimentation for a very, *very* rigid design, as even a single, minor change in the script would break several spells simultaneously, unless carefully done."

Caitlin's crisp voice continued

"Thankfully, the design is modular. We have done six here, both because hexagons work symmetrically with triangles and because six is usually more than enough separate temperatures for smithy work. It *can* be done with more, though dividing the shape into regular portions then requires more…unorthodox arrangements. Significantly riskier, and with little potential benefit."

"Aye, I can see that. You…could just do a second, or really up to six, linked hexagons, though, couldn't you?"

Caitlin's voice lost some of its edge. "Indeed, that is in fact known as Bryagh's Castle. You lose the ability to set based off the centre hex, but gain each of the surrounding hexes. Do *not*, I will note, do so in unbalanced arrangements. Opposite pairs are fine, two hexes on one side and three on the other is *not*. At least, if you wish to keep the anvil in its current shape."

"Power flow imbalance starts leaving residual heat on the overbalanced side, it eventually melts part of the script, and you have a runaway heat transfer with the power of a whole forge fire behind it?"

"Mm, more or less, though there *are* ways of counteracting, but none easier than just properly balancing it in the first place. You have the basics, now to the work that took even *me* weeks to sort out. We'll see how much you absorb in half a day. Do you see here where I modified the script to account for the existing anvil? And on this layer here where the same script meant I had to adjust this linkage accordingly, which cascaded another change to the adjacent triangle?"

Some hours later, Hannah's voice came in to the house where Leyla was just finishing re-etching a ward. "Apprentice Leyla, Chiefsmith Quinn, we should have the anvil all sorted."

"Ahem. *I* have sorted the anvil. Hedge Wizard Hannah now wishes to see if she got her silvers' worth."

Hannah gave a soundless sigh, and the smith and her daughter filed in for the demonstration.

"Now, just as with your existing anvil, you have a rack here. One of your peons informed me this was a convenient space, and I assumed he would not have dared do so without your prior approval. Now, simply place the index key"—Caitlin handed over a small token, shaped like an idealised anvil—"on the rack position for the temperature you desire, and the enchantment will heat any iron that you key to the anvil accordingly. Assuming you have sufficient heat in your forge, of course."

She finished by tapping a small spell carved into the stone next to the rack. "I see you have placed your keying sigil already, and indeed it uses the same framework as your existing anvil. Anything tapped on either sigil should work equally well for either anvil, which I'm sure will relieve your…associates."

Quinn's face was expressionless as she called to the bellows girl to pump the fire up, picked up an iron bar with her tongs, tapped the keying sigil, and placed it on the anvil. It immediately began heating, and then stopped on reaching a dull red colour. She repeated the test for each rack position, moving the token in order, until on her final test she had a white-hot bar.

"Well, Mage Caitlin, your work is as good as always. I've got your coin here."

She hefted a pouch, then poured the coins out before handing them over. "Seeing as you already have a purse, and all."

Quinn's eyes glinted. "I see I have transgressed against some *dire* rule of country politeness, for which I am *completely* heartbroken." She dropped the coins in to her purse one by one as she turned to Hannah with a raised brow. "And you? Are you satisfied with your purchase as well?"

Hannah nodded. "That I am, and I thank you for showing me. Now that I see how it works, I think there's all kinds of things I can use that technique for, at least simpler versions."

"You know, I nearly believe you. Farewell, Wagesmith, Hedge Wizard...oh, and Apprentice. With luck, we won't see each other again."

And with that, the mage stalked off.

Hannah waited until she was out of sight and hearing before taking a deep breath, and letting it out slowly. Quinn wrapped an arm around her shoulders.

"You did well, Hannah. Putting up with all that's no easy thing, but you're well on your way to being a better wizard than Aoife ever was, and she'd be right proud of that."

Hannah snorted. "Aunt Aoife never would have put up with such *cheek. Chief*smith."

Quinn nodded. "Aye, that's so. And she never learned anvil-enchanting, either, now did she?"

"Hm."

The wizard ruminated a moment, before her daughter walked up and enfolded her in a hug. "Well, *I* think you did wonderfully, Mama. We could tell she wasn't as hoity-toity when she was talking *with* you instead of talking *at* you, which must mean *something*, right?"

Hannah absently ruffled Leyla's hair. "Aye, it does. Just…not as much as I hoped it would. And she would never have done that much if she weren't desperate, she's definitely come down in the world. What a real, proper University mage would think…"

She shook her head, before nodding thanks to Quinn. "But you're not wrong, I got what I needed, and I've done worse for less. Though that's a pile of silver I won't see again anytime soon."

Quinn gave a little smile. "Oh, perhaps. Then again, perhaps not. I know I wouldn't care to bet on that. But away with you, your husband'll be waiting."

Hannah nodded, and gathered up her things. "That he will. You…" Hannah paused. "You should come by for supper sometime, Quinn. We don't see enough of each other."

The smith's smile broadened. "Well, as it happens I was just thinking the same thing. Ever since Aoife's passing, I've been a little too focused on my forge, I think. You just tell me the day and I'll be there."

Hannah smiled back, nodded, and started for home. Leyla followed close behind, staying quiet for as long as she could.

"Mama, is there a reason we haven't had Great Aunt Quinn over before? She always was nice to me, whenever I went to market with Papa or I saw her at the festivals."

"Ah, Ley-ley…when your great aunt Aoife died, it was hard on me, even though I'd finished my apprenticeship by then. But it was harder on Quinn. She didn't wail or weep, she just…stayed longer at the smithy, working by forge-light and feel. Some griefs are too private to talk about, and she's not an easy woman to bring things up to. I'm glad I tried today, though."

"Me too! She can throw me even higher than Papa can." Leyla nodded firmly.

Hannah grinned. "Well, can't argue with that. But why don't you run ahead, go greet that Papa with his low-throwing arms?"

"My *what* arms?"

Ciaran's outraged voice didn't so much float down the walk as drop down it.

"I'll let your daughter explain *that* one, Cirie. I'm plain worn out from that *mage*. But…we'll be having Quinn to supper, sometime."

Her husband's surprised nod was somewhat sideways as he tossed his giggling daughter towards the sky. "Good. I'll have to put a nice pie together for her then. And if certain *someones* are willing to recant these *slanders* on my arms, they might get to enjoy a slice or two themselves."

Hannah caught Leyla and set her down, wrapping Ciaran's arms around her own shoulders. "I recant any and all slanders, as long as they're *hugging* arms for a bit."

Ciaran smiled, and then laughed as Leyla wiggled herself between them to claim her spot.

"I can hardly argue with that. But before we get *too* wrapped up—"

Leyla chirped "Too late!"

"Welcome home."

Bug Hunting

Hannah listened to the wind and rain blustering against the side of the house, and shook her head. "April's borrowing days came due, all right. Not looking forward to the walk down to old Blair's place in *this*."

Leyla nodded glumly. "Me neither, Mama. Do you think singing it might make old March a little happier with us?"

Hannah smiled at the hope in her daughter's voice. They'd been too tired to do as much singing together lately, but with planting season finally trailing off they should get back to that. "Can't hurt, might help, let's give it a try."

They kept it quiet so they wouldn't wake Ciaran as they finished putting boots and cloaks on.

Old March said to fair April
I see three lambs on yonder hill
Three days auld-style you give to me
They'll leap no more, I guarantee

That first day was wind and wet
The second of them the snow upset
The third of them was such a freeze
It froze the birds right to the trees

But when the days were past and gone
The shepherds watched until the dawn
With many a curse, and many a yawn
But three wee lambs still leapt along

They were both smiling by the time they finished and they had finished their preparations, such as they were, for the weather ahead. Hannah gave her daughter a little squeeze. "Let's see if we can manage as well as the lambs, Ley-ley. Out we go!"

The struggle began immediately. Even getting the door closed again was a trial, and they were buffeted all the way down the walk. The rain was practically horizontal at points, and Hannah was just glad their cloaks stood up so well against it, though even the heavy fabric flapped in a gust and let the rain in. By the time they made it to the fullery, both of them were cold, wet, battered, and exhausted. Hannah had to push with no little effort to shove the door closed again, and that was *with* Leyla helping.

"Well, lassies, did the borrowing days leave you in one piece? Still able to leap and gambol?"

Hannah took a deep breath as she turned, and immediately regretted it as the various stenches, not least of which was that of stale urine, finally registered on her nose. She managed to only cough once before waving to the sharp old woman addressing them, though she could hear that Leyla wasn't quite as lucky.

"Still in one piece, Fuller Blair, still in one piece."

"Good! Don't worry about the smell, you'll be used to it soon enough, and it'll make your return trip all the more pleasant for it, hah!" Blair tapped her walking stick on the floor for emphasis.

"She's right, Apprentice, leastwise I know I've always enjoyed the walks back after a visit here."

Leyla had finally gotten her coughing under control, but her eyes were still watering and her nose was running a bit. "I'm sorry, Fuller Blair, I just wasn't expecting it."

"No matter, as long as you can do what needs doing that's enough for me. Come along!" She waved imperiously with one hand while she walked, stick tapping evenly. The various workers would sometimes pause and greet Hannah and Leyla as they made their way through the workshop, but most were too occupied (or at least making a point of showing they were, as Blair eyed them) to pay them any mind.

Blair's stick eventually tapped on a long wall on the far side of the workshop from the river and the two different waterwheels that powered the fullery. The wall was almost completely covered in one enormous spell, script stretching from Hannah's shins to a bit above her head. Hannah gave a low whistle.

"You've added a fair bit to the wool-sorter since the last time I was in here, Fuller, that's some nice work."

"Of course it is! Just because I'm not a wizard doesn't mean I don't know the spells for my own craft better than you ever will." Blair hmphed, glaring up and daring Hannah to disagree.

"But since I can't be *everywhere*, I've been leaving some of this to one of the feckless youths I *thought* I had trained properly, except the fool boy has *somehow* added a spellgram that sorts colours better and also makes it so the flooded thing can't tell the difference between wool and *kemp* half the time! I'd sort it out myself, but the engineers for the third waterwheel we're planning are barely out of swaddling clothes and I'm needed there more than here."

A sheepish young man had approached during this, and bobbed his head shyly at Hannah and waved to Leyla. Hannah gave a sympathetic smile along with her return nod; Leyla was too tickled at a respectable old woman swearing to notice.

"I trust a wizard can sort out his mess, and if the stars bless me maybe you can teach him to *test* properly before he carves his latest bright idea into the wall." Blair sniffed and stalked away.

After waiting until she was out of earshot, the man spoke up. "Good to see you, Wizard Hannah, Apprentice Leyla, though I wish it were under better circumstances. I really have *no* idea how the spellgram went so wrong—it worked fine when I tested it on its own, but somehow, as a part of the larger spell, it just…" He shrugged helplessly.

"It's all right, Apprentice Hamish, we'll sort it out. Something this big, that's going to happen every now and then, no matter how careful you are. At least the problem is *obvious*—sometimes you'll get one that you don't notice until all kinds of other changes have been made, then you have the *worst* time trying to untangle it all."

"There is that, and…thank you. It's been a bit of a rough time, the last few days."

Hannah could imagine. Blair Harper was not one to suffer fools gladly, and despite the smell the high pay at the fullery meant she had enough leverage not to have to.

"Let's start with the spellgram itself, hm? I know you tested it, but never hurts to start with the *easy* things first."

They spent the next several minutes doing just that. Like most spells of this size, the wool-sorting spell was divided into various spellgrams that each had their own self-contained functions. The one they were looking at was supposed to handle colour sorting, another handled fibre length, a third looked at texture, and so on. The fundamental design of the spell was such that none of the spellgrams should interfere with each other. As Hannah noted, though, "should" was the right word.

"It's not like you can tell the *spell* that each one of these is separate, the magic just does what you tell it to." She was speaking more loudly than usual, as was everyone else in the fullery, to make sure they were heard over the constant sound of the wheel-powered hammers pounding in the background.

"Well, yes, but each of the spellgrams is set with precedence, and nothing in mine should have priority over anything in the fibre-selector. That takes precedence over *everything.*"

Hannah mulled over the script. The tests on the colour-selector on its own had worked fine, as expected. She looked down to ask Leyla a question, and saw her daughter was looking withdrawn. "Something wrong, Apprentice?"

Leyla winced a little, and spoke quietly, too quietly for Hannah to hear.

"Couldn't quite catch that, can you speak up a bit?"

Leyla's mouth opened, and then she shook her head before saying more clearly, "It's nothing, Wizard Hannah."

Her mother noted that, and the wizard filed it away for future reference. "Well, Apprentice Hamish, nothing for it. We're going to have to some tests of the whole thing and go bug hunting."

Leyla nodded, and Hamish tilted his head in confusion.

"Ah, sorry, it's a wizard thing. One of the most common reasons spells go wrong is bugs have been nibbling or whatever else they do on 'em, so when we're trying to find what's making a spell go sideways, we call it bug hunting. There are all kinds of different 'bugs' we end up finding besides literal ones, but the name stuck."

The next hour was spent doing every different kind of test Hannah could think of, trying to isolate down the bug. The theory was if they could find the exact scenario that caused the kemp (and as they tested, the hair as well) to not get sorted out from the wool, that would give them a much better idea of where in the script they needed to look for the problem.

They settled into a routine division of labour. Hamish took different clumps of fibres and dropped them into the funnel, Leyla called out what the results were, and Hannah made notes about what combinations were correctly sorted, and which weren't. Finally, she nodded.

"That last test settles it, then. When the colours are all pretty close, everything works fine, it's when the wool is *very* different colours that the problem happens. Most likely, if you were doing everything from one sheep, you'd never notice an issue, but if you were mixing different types together, that'd be where you'd see it."

Hamish nodded. "That makes sense. We first saw it when we were emptying out the last of the dregs from storage to make room for the new shearing. Would have been lots of different small batches."

Leyla was uncharacteristically quiet, and her mother made another note. Nothing to be done about that now, but later…

"Okay, so, that give us some clues. Now, let's look at the script, circle by circle."

Like most spells, each of the spellgrams here were done in concentric circles, with the innermost circles being the most fundamental, and each expanding ring modifying them in some fashion. Everything looked normal on the first pass, and Hannah and Leyla couldn't see anything amiss.

"Not surprising, I suppose, if it was obvious you'd have caught it by now…"

Hannah mulled it over silently for a bit before calling out, "Hamish, what was it that your improvement was supposed to do, again?"

"Oh, it improved the efficiency. We were occasionally burning more power than the waterwheel could provide, and getting erratic results, with some of the more tangled batches. After some testing I realised the colour-sorter was burning more than I would have thought, and rewrote the outer two circles. That fixed the efficiency issue, but…"

He gestured at the short, brittle kemp fibres still mixed in with the wool. Hannah nodded.

"Why did it end up being more efficient?"

Hamish blinked. "I…don't really know. It just was."

Hannah grinned. "Ah, *there* we go. Apprentice Leyla, can you tell me why that's important?"

Leyla just shook her head, staring down at her feet. Hannah frowned before continuing.

"Well, that's all right, it's not the simplest thing ever. But when something uses less power, and you don't know *why*, that's a sign that the spell's behaving in a way you're not expecting. Let's take a look again, looking for anything that looks *too* simple."

"Too simple, Wizard Hannah?"

"Aye. It'll be easier to explain if we have an example, so let's see if we can find one before I try to explain."

Hannah and Hamish both began pouring over the spellgram again, while Leyla hung back. Eventually, Hannah vented a short "Hah!" and pointed. "We'll have to test it, but I think *this* is your problem."

Hamish peered at it, voice uncertain. "That's just a section saying that if the colour is *very* different, then we can skip the rest of the different types of checks for more subtle differences. How would *that* cause an issue?"

Hannah grinned. "Because it doesn't have the precedence-modifier on it. I'll bet it's not skipping the rest of the script *in this spellgram*. It's skipping the rest of the checks *in the spell*."

Hamish's mouth made an O of understanding, eyes widening. "Fire beside me and water around me, you're right!"

Hannah waggled her hand. "Probably, but let's test it first."

The testing took another half hour (and they discovered that it wasn't quite as simple as all that; there were two other minor bugs partially masking the issue), but they eventually had it. A few minutes of careful adjustment to the script later, with carving for new lines and resin filling old ones, and they were able to correctly sort any clump of fibres they could find.

Hamish went to go fetch Blair, and they had to run through the tests again for her. "Just as foolish as I expected, then. And what is the efficiency like now?"

"A bit better than it was before Apprentice Hamish's changes, Fuller Blair, but nowhere near as good as it was before just now. The 'improvement' was because almost the whole spell was being skipped, so it was mostly an illusion."

The old fuller gave an aggrieved sigh, and Hamish shrank in on himself. "So not only did you waste time, and make it so I had to call the wizard in, we don't even have anything to show for it? Oh, *well done*, Apprentice."

The acid dripping from that '*well done*' could have chewed through steel, and Hamish shrank further. Blair dismissed him with a brusque wave, and turned to Hannah directly. "At least the damage is done, now. I'll settle up with Ciaran, and you had best be going before your child is sick all over my clean floor. It's urine I need, not vomit."

Leyla flushed and looked down again. The wizard raised an eyebrow and her voice was hard. "I don't mind contending with a sharp tongue, but *my apprentice* is not yours to practice it on, Fuller."

Blair gave a short laugh. "My, my, my, Aoife's little waif *has* grown up, hasn't she? Fine, Wizard, you and your apprentice have my apologies for the uncalled-for remark."

Her grin was humourless.

"But this fullery *is* mine, young Wizard, and I want you out of it before that *relentlessly* polite husband of yours charges me for *more* of your time."

She jabbed with her stick towards the door, and Hannah gave a stiff nod and walked towards it, making sure Leyla was with her. As they left, Hannah could hear Blair beginning to lay into Hamish even over the sound of the hammers.

The wind, thankfully, had died down a bit while they were in the fullery. The rain had not, but after the close stench inside it felt cleansing.

They walked on for a good ways, Hannah gauging her moment, before asking bluntly "What's wrong, Ley-ley? And don't tell me 'nothing,' I can see something's up."

Leyla took a few more steps before answering, not looking at her mother. "I'm just stupid, that's all."

"Now where in the *world* did you get that idea from?"

The young girl sniffled. "I couldn't make sense of *anything* in the spell."

"Well, aye, it was some complicated work…"

"No! I mean, I just… It was so big, and then everything just looked like squiggles, and all I could do was look at *wool* fluff and how am I going to be a wizard when I can't even read *spells* and—"

Hannah's voice was cool. "Apprentice Leyla, do you think I'm an idiot?"

Leyla started, looking up at her mother for the first time since they left. "No, Wizard Hannah."

"It sure sounds like you do."

Leyla shook her head rapidly, spraying water droplets. "No, Mama, I don't! Why would you *say* that?"

"Because you seem to think after being an apprentice for less than a year, you should be as skilled at wizarding as I am a good"—Hannah had to pause to do the maths, and winced a little at the total—"twenty some-odd years after I started my apprenticeship."

Leyla was silent.

"And the only way *that* would be is if you were the kind of wizard songs were written of, and I was the kind of idiot who kept bumbling in front of that wizard like they have in those songs. Is that what you think of me, that I'm some blunderer like Thom, not seeing my life being stolen? Or the cyclops, fooled by nobody at all?"

Her daughter turned angrily, tears streaming down her face. "*No!* Stop being *mean*!"

Hannah kept walking through the rain. "I will, as soon as you stop being mean to yourself."

Leyla had to run to catch up. "I don't *understand!*"

Hannah turned and embraced her daughter. "Night-star, you're not *supposed* to. You're not *supposed* to understand everything yet. You're not *supposed* to be able to follow a spell so complex that old biddy couldn't make hide nor hair of it. And I don't care what she said, there's no world where she'd have brought us in if she thought she could have fixed it."

She squeezed, hard. "You're smart as anyone, smarter than most. But it takes *years* of working on this kind of thing to make sense of it all. I've only worked on spells that big a handful of times in my whole *life*, and haven't even read that much about them. They just don't come up all that often. And you know me, if I thought you should know something, I'd tell you."

Leyla squeezed back.

"Now, I'm going to put this down to the stink making you silly, all right? And if you think you're stupid on something, I want you to *talk* to me about it before it starts going round and round in your head. That's an order, Apprentice."

The voice that replied was muffled, but still understandable. "Understood, Wizard Hannah."

"Good! Now, let's get out of the wet, hm?"

Ciaran did not have the door open to greet them today, given the weather, but he was just inside it ready to take their cloaks, and with a steaming soup sending delicious smells through the air.

"Ooh, Papa, this smells *so* much better!"

He laughed as he hung the dripping cloaks up. "Faint praise, but I suppose I'll take it!"

His wife kissed him as she stood on one foot, struggling to get a boot off. "It would smell good even if we *hadn't* been in a fullery all day." Hannah gave him a significant look and a subtle nod toward Leyla, indicating they needed to talk more about their daughter later.

Ciaran widened his eyes briefly in acknowledgement before turning. "There, you see Ley-ley? Just a little change in how you word it, and the compliment shines all the brighter! I've had some blankets heating in front of the fire, and with a few hot stones in the middle to make sure they are cosy all around. Can't have my ladies catching cold, can I? But first!"

His strong arms swept them both off their feet, crushing them against his hearth-warmed chest.

"Welcome home."

Interlude: Summer Fair

"Oh *Papa*! Mama, come look at how *pretty* these are! And they fit so *well*!"

Smiling at her daughter's rapturous tones, Hannah draped an arm over her husband. It was good seeing Leyla so happy after that worrying episode at the fullery. She and Ciaran had talked about that more than once, and she'd been treading carefully trying to understand how she'd missed her daughter's distress so badly, but today was a day for joys rather than worries.

"Well, you earned them, Apprentice Leyla. A full year since you started your apprenticeship—formally, anyways—and you *are* owed a new set of clothes and all."

Leyla was holding up the new dress, looking over the brightly dyed reds and oranges, and exclaiming every time she found a new little pocket.

"Well of *course* you had to have plenty of pockets. Where else are you going to store little toads to surprise me with?" Ciaran's voice was only slightly wry. He had forgiven her for surprising him with rock toads after her trip to Blackhills. Mostly.

"Now, while she's distracted, here are *your* new clothes, love."

Hannah raised an eyebrow, unfolding the cloth until her breath caught. "Cirie, what… Are you *crazy*? We can't afford things this fine… Can we…?" She trailed off at her husband's smug look.

"Hannah, my most absentminded of wizards, not only can we afford it, but I've already topped off our charcoal bin from the winter, and I have a few other surprises for the Fair."

Ciaran's face drew more serious (or as serious as he could manage with Leyla excitedly chattering to one side), seeing the hesitant look on Hannah's face. "Hannahlan, you know your craft, trust I know mine. I know the planting season was gruelling, but with everything I've been able to sell, the commissions I could take in that time, plus the goods Captain Angelie traded us… We're doing better than we ever have." He tried to kiss the worry out of her face, which was as successful as it usually was. "Enjoy it, dearest. You've worked hard enough for it."

And so it was that their little family arrived at the Fairgrounds, set on a rolling hill that normally served for sheep grazing and far enough from the village to not risk burning anything important if a contest got out of hand. All three were wearing new clothes with bright colours, and brighter spirits. Each was carrying a large, covered woven basket holding either their picnic supplies for later or Ciaran's entry to the baking competition, and Hannah and Ciaran were each

wearing packs with wizardry supplies for the various con-
tests.

"It's a good thing it's the longest day of the year, Papa,
there's so much to *do*!"

Ciaran gently set his pack on the ground as Hannah
started setting up, and grinned back as he took Leyla's
basket from her. "It's almost like the Council planned it that
way, hm? Go, have some fun, just be back for the apprentice
competitions! Oh, and before I forget, you have your coin,
and here's how much you can barter away in middling-qual-
ity wool for spinning…"

He leaned down and ostentatiously whispered in her ear,
which proved to be a mistake as she squealed loudly at close
range. "*That much?* Oh, *Papa!* Mama, did I *really* earn that
much?"

Here, Hannah was on surer ground, as she and Ciaran
had settled on what Leyla had earned earlier in the week.
"That you did, Night-star, that you did."

The wizard wisely braced herself before her daughter
enthusiastically thanked her, before running off to one of the
nearby stalls. Hannah just smiled as Ciaran helped her with
the preparations. "We're doing all right with that one, aren't
we?"

"Of course we are! If we weren't, trust me, I'd have
heard about it from *every* busybody at the market."

Hannah rolled her eyes. The way he talked about the
markets, nothing would ever get *done* over the gossiping.
She was sure it couldn't be *that* bad… Though she wasn't
about to try taking his place haggling.

The next hour was devoted to setting up the various
competitions, and eyeing the different challenges. Hannah,
as the official wizard of Bywater, was in charge of running

the magical competition for the adults, as well as preparing a bit of showing off. All the wizards from nearby villages would be there, if they could, and while it wasn't an *official* competition, there was a bit of friendly rivalry in who had the most impressive demonstration.

Ciaran was competing in the baking contest, of course, and had an *impressively* decorated and filled pie for it, but was otherwise planning to relax and enjoy himself. Leyla was joining the older children in a hybrid contest that tested their ability to run, jump, and quickly (but *accurately*) chalk a spell, and of course had to be ready in case her lot was drawn for an animal later, but otherwise was free.

The Fair was growing busier by the minute, as people arrived from the outlying villages, and those who had come from downriver finished their own preparations, when Hannah finally nodded to Ciaran. "That should do it. It'll be interesting to see what everyone comes up with…"

He shaded his eyes as he looked up to the top of a tall pole they had fitted together. "Yes, it will. Getting the basket *down* is doable enough, but doing it without even cracking an egg? Tricky indeed…"

It would be some time before the competition itself, and Hannah and Ciaran decided to go watch the sheep shearing. It was early enough that there might still be some amusing mishaps, before the real experts settled down for the main event later. Leyla had watched for a bit, giggling as one of the sheep escaped an irate shearer, but by this point was enraptured by a small troupe of players who had come upriver.

"Come! Sit! And we shall tell you the tale of Merian Twice-Orphaned, and her bloody revenge against the Brass Monarchs and their arrogant warriors!"

Leyla knew the story, of course. Everyone in the Free Rivers did. But seeing performers act it out with their strange garb and heartrending music was another experience *entirely*.

"Our tale begins with Merian, adopted in the peace-loving village of Winter's Ease after a flood destroyed her first home. Seeing strange sails on the horizon..."

Leyla and the crowed ooh'd and aah'd over the wondrous silks, golden ornaments, and strange spices the "traders" brought to Winter's Ease, and were appropriately horrified at the wicked betrayal that night as the poor villagers were slaughtered in their beds. Only Merian, hearing the barest whisper of a gasp from her dying mother, managed to flee in time, killing two with a cutting spell that left them clutching their throats, and her drenched in black blood in the moonlight.

"And as she hid in the forest, she swore then that her parents and adopted kin would be avenged, and the last thing the *traitors* would hear would be the names of those they murdered!"

The next part of the tale was the best, for everyone had different adventures for Merian on her quest for vengeance. This troupe had chosen to have her spend a season learning deeper spellcraft from the Queen of Queens, eating honey and learning the strange magic of the hives until she was half a Queen herself. And, indeed, some enterprising wizard in the troupe had a hive of bees dancing around the grim actor playing Merian, before finally assembling into an entourage that followed her north. Leyla was impressed—that was subtle magic. Maybe she should go get her mother...

"But now, Intrepid Merian encountered the carnage of the next village lost to the Bloody Wake of the Monarchs!"

Leyla was lost in the horror as Merian discovered *another* village ravaged. One woman, near death, held on only long enough to tell Merian her tale of woe, so similar to the heroine's own.

"But one final detail was new to Merian: The silks were false, only the barest scrap of true-silk over rags; the faintest hint of spices to cover common sawdust; and the merest sheen of gold over common brass! And their leaders called themselves the Queen and King of Gold, but Merian cursed them and proclaimed that before she was done, all the world would know them only as the *Monarchs of Brass*!"

She travelled up the coast, and the troupe showed a mastery of quick-changes, with villagers, merchants, sailors, and at last the citizens of the City of Brass to the far north all being played convincingly (to Leyla's wonderstruck eyes, at least) by the same half-dozen troupers.

"And here, Brave Merian nearly despaired, for she saw the wide expanse of the city, and all sworn to protect the *raiders* who brought them such wealth and plunder! But her bees encouraged her, and she turned her thoughts to what might bring such a den of iniquity low…"

The tale turned to her various attempts to take her revenge, each succeeding in killing some but being foiled by their canny wards and greater numbers. Until, of course…

"One frosted night, Merian shivered, unused to the harshness of northern winters. But as she slumbered uneasily, a dream came to her of the Lady of the Forest. The Lady knew of her travails, and wept with Merian at seeing her vengeance thwarted. And offered to her a dark bargain…"

Leyla shivered herself. Much of the tale was fanciful, she knew. But this part…was too plausible to ever be heard lightly. It was exaggerated, of course, but…

"All winter, and spring, and even summer, Merian spent drawing her great spell. Tying in each tree and shrub, each hive and den. And when the monarchs and their accursed reavers returned again for the great autumn feast and bonfire, Merian struck, closing the last line of the spell with her own blood."

"The bonfire grew higher, and higher, before *exploding* with a conflagration so great their wards could not contain it! Burning so hotly, that charred skeletons were seared to their brass thrones! And so widely that *none* in the city lived to tell the tale. And in the instant before their Doom came upon them, all heard Merian's voice echoing."

It seemed to Leyla that Merian herself, dripping with blood and harrowed with hate, spoke through the actor.

"Twice have I been orphaned, twice have I fled. Twice have I wept and wailed in darkest grief, and my only regret now is that I can kill you but *once*. For Winter's Ease, for all who trusted your twisted words."

All the music ceased, abruptly as a cut cord.

"*For Lauren and Lysette.*"

And with the names of her parents spoken, Merian too perished. Or so it seemed.

"For now, her bargain with the Lady of the Forest came due. In her wrath, Merian's great spell had consumed the forest entire. Ashes drifted in what had once been groves, fat crackled in what had once been flesh, and steam broiled away from what had once been streams, so searing had the consumption of the forest been."

"Merian, or what had *once* been Merian, began her ghoulish work. She was bound, bound until the forest was regrown, bound to take the corpses of any human who dared settle in the City of Brass, and plant seeds in them. Some say you can hear her when the wind blows in the north, luring the foolish to their demise. But I, I have been to the Blood-Grown Woods, and I tell you true that the trees there bear faces, locked in anguish. And so perhaps Merian *will* have the joy of seeing her tormentors die twice, after all."

As was traditional, there was no applause, no cheering at the end of the Tale of Merian Twice-Orphaned. But promises to buy food, and drink, offers of wool or mutton, and even a few coins were offered to the players. Leyla considered for a moment, and put a half-silver in the hand of Merian. She had *earned* it.

In the meantime, a few competitors had stepped forth to try Hannah's challenge. The first set a small scrap of circular wood around the pole, snapping it closed with a simple latch. He then closed the activation line on the spell, sending it up with the strength of his person alone. His little scrap made it to the top of the pole, but unfortunately spun uselessly there, whatever plan he had to get the "nest" down foiled. He broke the activation line on the spell near him, half-collapsing from the effort, as his scrap of wood fell to the earth.

The second had better luck, with an improvised setup involving another latched circle and a baking paddle. That succeeded in getting the entire nest onto the paddle itself with a cleverly timed wind spell, but she had overestimated her strength and Hannah called an end to the attempt as the woman began shivering in a thankfully mild case of spell-shakes. Her friends hauled her off to a warm blanket by the fire and some hot soup, with a promise that one of them would fetch Hannah if she got worse.

The third, though, just grinned up at the wizard cheekily. "I'm old enough, I swears!"

What were clearly her parents just shrugged helpless agreement, clearly agreeing that their daughter was old enough to qualify despite their better judgement. Hannah shrugged back. Some sixteen-year-olds *were* small for their age, though it was less common for girls.

The young woman set up her spells, scratched the activation line closed with her belt knife, and then chucked a rock at the nest. Hannah raised a brow as it flipped violently over, and then her other brow as a wind roared up to catch the three eggs, lowering them feather-light to the ground. Hannah inspected the eggs before nodding approval as the crowd cheered and lifted up the exhausted young woman onto their shoulders.

"Well, Zoey Clearwater, that was won fair and square. Here's your prize, and try not to pass out, aye?"

Hannah handed up a blue ribbon, and Zoey clutched it contentedly. She knew full well she wouldn't be buying her own drinks for the rest of the Fair, and likely not for a while to come, and to her that ribbon was worth more than a fistful of silver as she let her supporters haul her off. Her parents, bemused, just thanked Hannah for an interesting contest and went to go make sure she got *food* with that drink.

"And now it's time for the Wizard Exhibition!"

Hannah lightly punched Ciaran's shoulder. "You *know* I don't like it when you call it that. Makes me feel like a prize heifer about to be displayed."

Ciaran's grin was wicked. "Well, if you want to be on *display…*"

She hit him considerably harder this time, and he relented with a laugh. "Ooh, right, I will be good…for now, at least."

She rolled her eyes. That was as much as she was likely to get… And besides, she needed to *focus*. She was the last wizard to arrive, and the demonstrations began as soon as she took her place and nodded.

There were only four wizards, including her, showing this time, and the various apprentices had spent a good chunk of yesterday preparing wood piles for each of them to power their spells. A sizeable crowd was gathered, as this was almost as good as the travelling players.

The first, Skye Law of Berrywoods, stepped forth, dragging a line with her boot from a woodpile to the centre of the dirt, all the grass having been cleared a good ways around for *this*. She laid out a cloth with *very* intricate spells stitched on to it, and chalked the activation line closed. Her wood pile only started being consumed slowly, and there was no other obvious effect. The crowd murmured curiously.

Skye grinned, and walked toward one of the big fires that had been roasting animals since before dawn for the Fairgoers. And then, with a gasp from the crowd, she walked *into* the fire.

The moment she stepped in, her wood pile began shrinking noticeably as logs began flaring into ash. Hannah gauged the rate of burn, and then turned back to where Skye was merrily dancing, kicking up embers, and then leaning against the mutton dripping into the flames, making a point of appearing relaxed. She sauntered out a few seconds later, casually dusting herself while showing off that not only was she not burned, but no ash, no searing fat, *nothing* had stuck to her from her sojourn in the flames.

Hannah joined the applause, as did Ciaran and Leyla (who was now sitting on her father's shoulders to better enjoy the show). Hannah murmured back to Ciaran, "Show-off. Look at how much wood was burned for that, she could have danced in there another whole minute if she'd been willing to get a little ashy."

"That *is* the point of all this, dear. Showing off? Remember?"

"Aye, aye, but still. Sloppy."

She could see the next wizard shared her feelings, as Evan Dawson of Oak Landing rolled his eyes a little as he stepped forward. He used a walking staff to more precisely draw a line from his woodpile to the centre, and when he unrolled his spellcloth he ostentatiously double-checked it before closing the activation line. When he did, his wood pile did nothing, but he smiled anyway.

He nodded to an apprentice, who lit a torch before stepping forward and planting it in the dirt. Evan raised his hand, and pinched his fingers together. And just like that, the fire on the torch died, as his wood pile suddenly flared. This drew suitably impressed noises from the crowd, and he invited others to bring fire for him to douse (though no water seemed to be involved), and it took the third one before Hannah finally understood.

"Oho ho, he's not putting anything on the fire, he's moving the air *away* from the fire. The pinching motion is a distraction, aye... Not bad, Evan, not bad."

After proving that he could do (somewhat) larger fires at various distances, he bowed and returned to his place to a good smattering of applause. Hannah's was considerably louder this time, though the audience overall didn't seem as impressed.

"Getting the spell to pay attention to where he was looking and the motion of his hands is way, *way* harder than just moving the air away, Cirie, Ley-ley. I'll have to pick his brain on that, seemed pretty efficient..."

The third wizard stepped forward, and Marcus Holmes of Siltbend did *not* draw a line from his woodpile. Hannah covered her mouth with her hand. *This* should be good…

Marcus struck a pose, bringing his wrists together and showing the elaborate spellwork on his shirt in the early afternoon sun. He then drew them apart in a broad circle, and the crowd gasped as he left a vertical ring of fire hanging in the air. His wood pile was burning at a prodigious rate, but he jumped through the circle, fire trailing from his hands, and took a bow before cutting a thread binding the cuff of his shirt tightly against him, at which point the fire disappeared and the bare remnants of his woodpile ceased flaring.

The crowd roared approval, as Hannah hid her laughter. She could see Evan doing the same, and even Skye appeared amused. "That seemed pretty impressive, Mama…?"

"Aye, it sure *seemed* that way. But that's the most *inefficient* way of doing that, I could imagine. But, that's Marcus, all right, and now it's *my* turn."

Hannah strode out now, dragging a line with her own staff. Instead of unrolling a cloth as the other three had done, however, she unfolded a large stencil she'd had Ciaran put together for her, and quickly used her knife to cut a much less elaborate spell than the others into the dirt. She could hear the muttering from the crowd who had expected something faster, and just grinned.

She checked it once, and twice, before lifting the stencil, sticking her staff firmly into the ground in the middle of the spell, and drawing the final activation line with her boot. Her woodpile began flaring immediately, and she took several steps back. Her hair began to rise, and she could hear occasional noises of confusion, quickly hushed.

It was over in an instant, a brief flash that caused everyone to blink as the sharp *crack* of thunder rolled over them, startling those in other parts of the Fair. Hannah strode up and pulled the staff from the dirt, no worse for the experience, and her wood pile stopped flaring as she took a bow.

This time the applause was more gradual, as everyone took in what happened, but it grew and grew as Ciaran and Leyla ran up to hug her.

"My mama called *lightning*!"

She grinned as her husband stared at her in astonishment. "What, didn't you know what all you were making for me?"

"Of *course* not, I just make them, I don't *understand* all of them!"

"Well, you always *did* say seeing me at that first Fair was like a bolt out of the blue..."

"That's an expression!"

Hannah just laughed, and the whole event dissolved into people asking questions, buying drinks for the wizards, and enough excited chatter to make the thunder seem quiet. The wizards themselves traded words, with the rest making gentle fun of Marcus for his antics ("What? We're supposed to be *crowd-pleasers* for this!") and everyone promising to send their stencils around before the Fair broke up.

Eventually, a loud voice cut through the commotion. "All gather for the drawing of lots! It is time for the drawing of lots!" The same words could be heard more distantly, shouted at other places around the Fair. *That* dampened the excitement, and everyone began speaking more quietly as they filtered toward the main cookfires.

The meat that had been roasting since the early morning was essentially done, and the spits were cleared for the next round, with the animals for them waiting uneasily nearby. Once the rest of the Fair had been emptied, councillors from the various villages went around with sacks of beans. Most drew a bean and the councillor moved on, but a few drew and moved to follow the councillor.

Hannah drew a black bean, as did Ciaran. Leyla, however, drew a white bean, and gulped and paled as she followed. Ciaran's hand nearly crushed his wife's as they silently watched their daughter move to the front of the crowd. After all had been chosen, the spokeswoman called out to a silent crowd.

"This year, as every year, we give thanks. We give thanks that we have survived the winter frosts, and the spring floods. We give thanks that our fish thrive, and our sheep multiply.

"And we give thanks that we are free to enjoy all of these things. That we are safe from monarchs, safe from *bandits*, safe from any who might seek to deprive us of all that we hold dear.

"But that freedom has a cost, and we pay it now in token. All of us, from the children barely beginning their apprenticeships to elders barely able to hobble, must know the spells of defence. The spells of cutting. The spells of killing.

"And now, chosen by lot as we have always done, we will *demonstrate* that knowledge. For as long as we all can kill to defend ourselves, we *all* will be safe from those who wish to conquer us."

The spokeswoman nodded, and Leyla stooped to draw a spell along with the others who had drawn white beans. These spells alone were *always* done freehand, for an enemy might destroy stencils and clothing. These spells alone were *always* powered by a person's own strength, for an enemy might strike when no other source of power was available.

Leyla finished her spell, checked it once, checked it twice, and plucked a hair from the cow she was appointed to. The adults had to do it without the link, but children were allowed to use one. She placed it in the middle of the script, and closed the activation line.

She collapsed to her hands and knees, *carefully* away from the spell script, as the blood spurted from the cut artery on the cow and she felt her exhaustion overcome her. The spokeswoman of the councils nodded, and her parents rushed to pick her up, carrying her back. This year, as almost every year, the ritual was completed without incident. All those chosen by lot slew their animals, and all was well. No one liked to think about what happened when someone failed their part.

"All have proven that they can do their duty, and for that, we must *all* be grateful."

The spokeswoman's voice shifted from hard flint to relieved happiness. "And now, let's *really* get this celebration going!"

The crowd shouted, the tension funnelling into all their voices as it released, and the animals were hastily cleaned and added to the spits. Everyone drifted apart, and Hannah and Ciaran fussed over their daughter.

"Well, now, you did well, Leyla. You did well. Not everyone gets picked so young; you made us both very proud. We'll get some more food and drink into you; that'll help you feel better right soon."

Leyla yawned. "Okay, Mama, just…glad I did it…"

"Here, I think this is a good time for the last surprise, loves…"

Ciaran cradled Leyla carefully, only the barest hint of a tremble betraying his still-dissipating fear from earlier, and the family made their way to a small table by the cookfires. At his signal, a couple of adolescents approached and soon their table was laden with meat and flatbreads, as well as a clay pitcher.

"What is…Ciaran, a whole pitcher of elderflower cordial?"

"*Diluted* cordial, but yes. I was *planning* to save it for later, but I think Leyla's earned it."

Leyla perked up.

"Oh, *wow* Papa. How much can I have?"

Ciaran's smile made Hannah's heart hurt. "Today, Nightstar, you can have the whole pitcher if you want."

Leyla did not have to be told twice, and before long the food and drink had her ready to run around again. Soon enough she ran off to see what else the performing troupe had, and her parents wandered on their own, occasionally chatting with friends, but drifting towards the outskirts of the Fair proper.

"Well. We're all a whole year older, now. What a way to usher in her eleventh year…"

"Hush, Cirie. She's stronger than you think she is. I see it more these days, I knew she could do it."

"Mm. Well, that certainly put paid to my plan of finding a dark corner with you tonight, regardless."

Hannah nodded, squeezing her husband's hand. "Aye."

They walked for a time, letting the bustle wash over them. Eventually, Hannah shook her head, grinning at Ciaran. "Come on, we have to go see if you won *your* contest! Have to see if I should have married a different baker, after all."

Ciaran sniffed. "Hah, as if there was *any* chance I won't win. But certainly, let us go collect my prize, and if you're lucky, I'll even let you try the pie."

"Well, let's hurry then!"

Hannah grinned, and led the way.

Curing's Cure

"*Leyla Hendry*, if you wake your father with this *fool-ishness* then cowskins won't be the only hides I'll see tanned today. Outside, *now*."

Hannah's voice was quietly furious, and the severity of it cut through even Leyla's tantrum. Her daughter vibrated with outrage, but kept it suppressed long enough to stalk out the door and down the walk a good ways before she exploded again.

"*Why* do we have to go to the smelly tannery? I'm going to get stink all over my new *clothes*!"

"It was your choice to wear them today, nobody made you, and you knew full well where we were headed. Got no one to blame but yourself for that, *Apprentice*."

Leyla's voice went even shriller, though Hannah would not previously have thought that was possible. "I just *got* new clothes, of *course* I have to wear them! Just because *you* like running around in old clothes doesn't mean *I* do!

And what's the point of curing *hides* when we can heat metal without a *fire*? You called *lightning* and you want to get all mucky at a *tannery*? What kind of wizard *are* you?"

Hannah breathed in, breathed out, unclenched her fist one finger at a time, and loosened the hand on her walking stick. "A wizard who *works* for a living. Is calling lightning going to help get the sheep in, or the crops harvested? And we didn't heat metal *without* a fire, as you know full well. We just helped move the heat from a blazing fire. But most of the time, just heating it *on* the fire is better. We're going to 'get mucky' because that's what needs doing. They'll pay us well for our time, and we can use that to get plenty of food for the winter, more learning like we got at the smithy, and those *nice clothes* you keep harping about."

Only long practice helped Hannah keep her voice edged, rather than shouting right back. She was just congratulating herself on that when Leyla stomped ahead, turned a disdainful look over her shoulder, and spat, "Well, one day *I'm* going to be better than some *hedge wizard*."

For a moment, Hannah stopped, staring as her mind tried to wrap itself around what had just happened. There was a low sound that seemed to be coming from behind her ears, and that moment seemed to stretch as her heart tried to reconcile new rage and old humiliation and disappointment and who knew what else.

Leyla stopped, and the look on her face showed plainly that she knew she'd gone too far. She gave a small "Mama? I'm...I'm sorry, I didn't..."

Hannah's return was barely above a whisper, and edged with ice. "It's 'Wizard Hannah' today, Apprentice. And your father will see to you when we get home, because otherwise I'll do something I'd regret."

Leyla shrank. "Um, Wizard Hannah, I—"

She stopped at a sharp cutting motion from her mother. "Not. Another. Word."

The rest of the walk out towards the hills was through a fine summer day, warm with just enough of a breeze to be refreshing. Not that either of them noticed, of course.

By the time they saw the tannery, Hannah had herself under control, carefully setting aside her hurt until her husband had a chance to dress the wound later. What her daughter was feeling, she didn't know, and for the moment she didn't care. They had work to do, and that was that.

"Well, hello Wizard Hannah, Apprentice Leyla! You couldn't have picked a finer day to come visit us, and that's the truth!"

"Hello, Tanner Danny. And yes, it's a very nice day."

The elderly man raised an eyebrow at the flat words, and took in both of them before replying. "Well, at least it smells a good deal better than the last time you came by, thanks to that smell-trapper. Never could spare the power for the Guild spell, and we can even burn this charcoal when it's taken in all the stink it can hold. The whole Tanner clan thanks you kindly, and I think everyone at the market does too!"

He smiled as brightly as if his guests weren't stiff as two boards, the taller of whom winced at the mention of the word "Guild," and ushered them in. "But look at me gabbing, I know you are a busy woman, Wizard, so we can get right to it."

They followed him through a winding course between different vats—varying in colour and with hides at different stages of the tanning process in them—then around the mill grinding oak bark as the great blades far above caught wind to power the mechanism. It was an interesting sight, though both Hannah and Leyla's eyes were beginning to water, and Leyla sniffled before she immediately regretted it.

"Oh, that's right, it's much better than it was but still not what you would call smelling like flowers, I'm afraid. I'm sorry about that; I hope you'll be used to it soon enough and we *do* really appreciate all you've done, and hopefully *will* do, for us!"

"Paps is right, it's been a right blessing from sky above, or I guess fire within, what you did for us!"

An energetic young man paused from taking some hides from the drums they had just passed and putting them to soak in a barrel to remove the slaked lime, and waved enthusiastically. He seemed unperturbed at their halfhearted return waves as he focused again on making sure the acids did not splash out of the barrel.

"Here we are, yes, and I left the circular here so I wouldn't forget it. Now, Wizard, what do you make of this, hm?" He handed a sheet of printed paper over, indicating the relevant passage with a knobbly finger. Hannah mulled it over, reading it out loud to make sure this was what old Danny meant.

"*Experiments with an alternative curing method were initially promising, but we were unable to find a method more cost effective than traditional salt cures. The efficiency loss from magical assistance on the sunlight was unfortunately too large to overcome. Now, experiments in reducing the necessary time in the tanning vats to less than half previous durations—*"

"Nope, that's enough, Wizard Hannah, thankee kindly. It was the *curing* that caught my eye."

Hannah nodded, handing the page back. "So my husband told me, but I'm not quite sure why. If it's not any better than salting…?"

The old tanner grinned. "Well, now, I'm sure it's not, ways downriver and closer to the sea and all. And truth be told, it wouldn't be for us either, except salt's become a fair bit more dear lately."

"Aye, I think I heard Ciaran muttering something about that last market day."

"As we all have been! Some disaster or other down by the seaside; the river-folk have been talking of a great wave tall as a hill that swept half the coastline clean, as if we were to believe that!"

The three of them shook their heads, and Leyla's solemn disbelief made his eye twinkle. "Well, regardless of how gullible the river-folk think we are, it's clear there was some flood or likewise problem coast-ways. Which hasn't been all bad—they're paying for anything they can get their hands on, leather included, but it does mean salt's not as easy to come by as usual. And since they're paying premium for every scrap of leather they can get, well, I thought it might be worth trying to figure out this 'alternative curing method,' see how much we can tan and sell before they sort out the mess down there."

Hannah nodded, unstiffening a little as she got lost in the problem. "Fair enough, Tanner Danny, fair enough… They don't give us a *lot* to go off of though, do they?"

"Not a *great* deal, but the principle seems sound. Sun-curing can work, for some of the brightest days of summer, particularly up in the mountains I've heard. It's just not *reliable*, not anywhere near here anyways, and the leather you get from it isn't always the best quality even when it does work.

If we could improve on that, though… In any case, think it over—the Butcher lasses have a few beasts that should be skinned shortly and you can experiment with those. Won't be too large, just a few sheep, but I figure we can cut them into strips or suchlike."

Hannah nodded again, distracted as she started rummaging through her pack. "We'll see what we can figure, Tanner. Apprentice Leyla, I think you have some of the light stencils in your pack, can you find everything we have handy?"

Her thoughts caught up with her mouth, and she looked warily over. But Leyla just started handing over stencils—wordlessly, but handing them over all the same. Danny's brows drew together for a moment before his face cleared and he moved away. "Thankee again, both of you, and just give a shout if you need anything, one of us'll help with whatever. Oh, and I know this is asking a lot, but if you can find a way to make whatever this is work for hunters who've just skinned some game, then we'll be thanking you with a heavy purse indeed!"

Hannah managed a grin at that, and started to take a deep breath to call back before doubling over and coughing. A wave ended up being all she could manage before Danny disappeared.

"Right, deep breaths not a good plan, ayup. Now, how do you get more sunlight than you have…? Or, I guess, any other kind of curing that doesn't use salt, but I wouldn't even know where to start, there. And sunlight makes sense—everyone knows sunlight cleans all kinds of things, should stop rot just fine as well as drying the skin out…"

She sighed. She knew she was just stalling, and what the next step should be. "Let's go get some skins."

They made their way out of the tannery proper, and into the butchery adjoining it. Sure enough, some skins were ready, and Hannah almost managed to thank the amused Butcher twins without gagging. Leyla didn't even try to stop her own gags, even with a sharp look from her mother. At least they were then able to go outside, and upwind.

"Phew! Well, enjoy it while we can, I suppose. I'm just glad they started using that smell-trapper. Last time I was down here I plain lost my breakfast. And my lunch."

Her conversational gambit fell flat as Leyla pointedly ignored her, and Hannah felt another roil in those set-aside feelings. "Let's take a look at those stencils, Apprentice."

The next few hours were near-torture for Hannah. Leyla assisted, with the fewest possible words spoken, but Hannah missed the sounding board she'd grown accustomed to over the last year. She'd never worked much with light spells—they generally were simple enough that most who needed them did their own, and took too much power to be worth experimenting with most of the time. The stink lingered, even outside, and every time she coughed she could feel her daughter's eyes saying *I told you so.*

It was hard to tell, but she didn't *think* anything she was trying was making a difference. She knew it would be a full day before they knew for sure, and hours yet before there was even an obvious sign, which made the whole ordeal even more frustrating. Her grip on the chalk was so tight that eventually it snapped in half as she tried another attempt at putting more light to shine on the skins, and she gave a half-strangled scream of frustration, stalking off and staring up into the sky.

Later, she thanked that broken chalk, but right at the moment it seemed that everything was thwarting her *inten-*

tionally, even the sun itself, and she turned to give it a good glare as it floated behind a thick cloud. Of course, the cloud chose that moment to sail quickly, and she was blinded as the sun glared back.

"Oh, of all the *famined* things, I just can't—! I've been staring at twenty different light spells and *now* I get blinded? Sky above and ground below, I just—"

She stopped, pausing.

"…Huh. I *have* been staring at different light spells. And none of them were bright enough to be an issue…"

She slapped her forehead. It was so *obvious*. She scrambled back to her chalk, grimaced at the broken halves and made some cautious changes to her last attempt, wracking her memory for the half-forgotten script. Since she was forced to freehand, she triple-checked the spell and Leyla even stopped pouting long enough to check a fourth time, both agreeing that they couldn't see how the spell could cause real damage. Hannah pulled the smallest chunk of charcoal she could find to power the spell for the test. She had Leyla duck behind a tree with a ready water bucket, just in case. The charcoal flared immediately when she closed the activation line, and the spell itself flared sun-bright for an instant, leaving her eyes dazzled and watering.

"Hah! No one ever says *fire*light cleans wounds or linens, it's *sun*light that does that! Can't believe I remembered that spell; circular must have been half a dozen years ago…"

The sunlight spell was even more power-hungry than most light spells, which was saying something, so she couldn't do much of a test out here. Back inside, then, and she was too caught up in the grip of solving a problem to even notice the smell, at least when Leyla wasn't making a point of her own noticing.

"Tanner! I think I have something for you! But hoo-*boy* is it going to eat power like crazy. Probably be days of testing and fine-tuning and such, but I have to know if you even want to burn that kind of power on it first."

Danny loped back in a curious gait that seemed designed to avoid every vat and pole and implement in the tannery. "Well, now, that sounds promising, but what kind of power are we talking, Wizard?"

They fell to a detailed discussion, and Danny called a few other members of the family over. They eventually stopped the bark grinding and drew a jury-rigged power line from the millshaft to where they'd settled for on the sunlight spell. Light blazed as Hannah closed the activation line, and a few whistles echoed through the much-quieter tannery. She picked up the hasty stencil she'd carved for her improvised spell, and nodded. "That'll do, I think, and there's power to spare. It'll take some experimenting, but this should get you all the sunlight you need. We'll want to take advantage of *regular* sunlight as much as possible, so long term we'll want to get it outside, at least when it's dry…"

Discussions and planning for the next day took a while, but eventually old Danny was guiding them back out, beaming almost as brightly as the spell had earlier. "That should do it right enough, Wizard Hannah, and I'm as grateful as can be for it! If we can make this work, should be able to save enough coin that we can get a real Guild education for Murray and his sisters. Wouldn't that be something, a Guild-certified tanner for Bywater!"

Hannah's smile faltered, and while he didn't appear to notice, the tanner's next words made her think he might have.

"And you'll get your share, of course. I know it's been your dream that little Leyla here would be able to go to University, but you should think about your own Guild certification, Wizard Hannah, if you'll pardon an old man's advice. I know Aoife and your parents never could raise the coin for it, despite you passing the exams and all, but coin's a bit freer these days than it was twenty years back."

He nodded amiably at Leyla's wide eyes. "Oh, aye, didn't your mother ever tell you? Passed the exams, even beat out some of the children of the Guildmembers. You should be right proud of your mama, you should. I've always said she'd go far. Not many I'd trust freehan-ah, *improvising* a spell anywhere near my land, not at *all*, not sure I'd have even trusted old Aoife, but I trust Hannah."

He gave a creaky laugh while the wizard's face flushed. "Ah, but there I am jawing away again, I've got to let you be on your way, otherwise your good Papa will be cold at me next market day, and we don't want that!"

He shooed them out, and left a flustered pair to begin their walk home. The long summer afternoon was still bright, in a hazy golden way, and after the noisy and noisome day it was soothingly gentle. Hannah tried to soak it in, and just stop thinking for a time, and managed to even partially succeed.

They were nearly in sight of home when Leyla finally broke the silence. "I'm sorry, Wizard Hannah."

She took off running before her mother could respond, opening the door and marching up to her father, who had been taken aback by her speed. "Spellbinder Ciaran, I was very mean today and said things I shouldn't have and I know I can't take them back but I know I was wrong and I'll do whatever you say to make up for it and I'm sorry and that's that."

Leyla braced, as Ciaran tilted his head in confusion. He watched his wife walk slowly up, eyes bright with tears, and his brows drew down. "I see, Apprentice Leyla. We'll discuss that in a moment, but, no matter what, you are still my daughter. So, first—"

He wrapped a weeping Hannah in his arms, and felt Leyla gripping his leg, tears starting from her eyes as well. He moved one arm to give her a squeeze, before returning it to his wife's shuddering shoulders.

"Welcome home."

Family History

The late summer sun was not yet up as Hannah and Leyla tried to finish their breakfast. Both were bleary eyed, and they had just seen Ciaran off to bed.

"At least…Papa made a nice…*pie* for us to have for lunch." The yawns between Leyla's words set Hannah off again, and they were both yawning back and forth for a solid minute before she was able to respond.

"Aye, even if he *is* just trying to show my sister he's taking care of us, it'll still be a nice pie."

Leyla frowned at her mother as she struggled to settle her older (and lighter and shorter) cloak around her. "Aunt Rosie *knows* Papa takes good care of us. That can't be the *only* reason."

Hannah grinned as she slipped into her thankfully light pack and grabbed her walking stick. "Ley-ley, hardly anyone ever does *anything* for just *one* reason. But trying to make a show for my sister was certainly *a* reason we got this pie.

I'll just bet it's full of beef instead of mutton, and one of the fancy gravies he does."

Her eleven-year-old apprentice eyed the pie in the basket with new interest. "A *beef* pie? I don't even *remember* the last time we had beef."

The wizard laughed as she walked out the door, stick in one hand and basket in the other. "Sure you do, it was when Rosie stayed for dinner, must have been over a year ago, after the market day. We"—she broke off for another yawn—"*always* have something special when Rosie'll see."

They set off on the path towards Berrywoods, finishing waking up as the food and conversation finally convinced their heads that returning to bed wasn't going to happen this time. "She's the last family I've got left, and he's never gotten over your Grandda sniffing and asking what was burning the first time he cooked for my family. Makes a point of proving his cookery every chance he gets."

"But…Aunt Rosie doesn't even pay that much attention to food. She'll eat any old thing, if it's handy."

Hannah's grin widened. "Well, *I* know that, and *you* know that, but your *father* doesn't know that. And what your papa doesn't know won't stop us from having a special meal from time to time, will it?"

Leyla laughed. "I guess not, Mama!"

They walked a fair ways, the sun finally peeking over the hills, just talking. They talked about the upcoming harvest which would interrupt their usual work for a time, the birdsong above, the shine of the river like silver fish scales, whatever came to mind. Eventually, Hannah gauged they were only another hour away from her sister's.

"All right, Apprentice Leyla, let's review. We don't know what all the design will look like, so we'll have to fit bits and bobs of the spell wherever we can. What are the key components of the overall warming spell?"

Her daughter closed her eyes briefly, reciting. "Temperature checker, warmer, linker, and limiter."

"Ayup. And what are the sizes of each spellgram like? Relative size is good enough."

"Temperature checker's pretty big, so is the limiter. The linker is pretty small, and the warmer is about as small as it gets."

"Aye, it's kind of funny how the thing we *actually* want the spell to do is dead simple. It's getting it to do it the right way, safely, at the right *time*, that's hard."

Leyla nodded. "It's like that with a *lot* of spells, though. Most people just don't understand how complicated wizarding is."

She nodded again, firmly. Hannah grinned and nudged her with the basket. "And a good thing too! Otherwise how would we get work, and bring home enough barter for your father to make nice beef pies for us? But let's see, oh yes, what kind of shapes can we do the limiter spellgram in?"

"Circular, hexagonal, octagonal if we have a lot of space..."

They spent the rest of the walk pleasantly enough, Hannah desultorily drilling Leyla on all the variations she could think of for what was, in the end, a fairly simple spell. The temperature checker was mildly complicated, but only mildly, as it checked to see if it was cold enough to be worth activating. The limiter was big, but it was just there to make sure it didn't burn any more power than was needed to keep people under it from freezing, which wasn't terribly complicated when you already had a temperature checker.

Eventually they sighted the embroidery, and she let the drilling trail off as they approached in their usual fashion: Stealthily.

They crept up toward the haphazardly expanded building that Rosie and the rest of her circle both lived and worked out of, staying as quiet as possible. They then slipped inside, ostentatiously "sneaking," to the amusement of the other embroiderers. They in turn did their part by continuing their usual conversations and singing. The pair waited until Rosie set her crewel needle down to gather up the next heavy pricked paper for her design, and then lunged forward in an aggressive hug before she reached it.

Rosie, as always, squawked as the rest of the embroiderers laughed and cheered. "We *got* you, Aunt Rosie!"

"Because you are *nefarious* sorts! I just wish *one time* that you would greet me like a *person* instead of an oversized doll!"

Hannah squeezed her sister one last time before straightening up. "Well, where would the fun be in that? Besides, you like the game well enough when you catch us."

Rosie harrumphed, mock glaring at everyone else in the room. "I don't know *what* gave you such an impression, sister-dear, but you are *badly* mistaken. After all, if I enjoyed your silly game, then I might *also* enjoy *sudden tickle attacks*!"

Her clever fingers were wickedly employed then as she revenged herself on niece and sister. "Hah! *Now* you'll remember not to let your guard down!"

She spotted the gleam in their eyes and raised a finger. "Now, now, turnabout is fair play, and if we don't start working then we'll be at this for ages."

Hannah and Leyla reluctantly conceded the point, and after a few greetings with the rest of the embroiderers, settled down to business. "Fair enough, sister mine. Now, let's see your quilt."

The *large* twill quilt laid out before them was already a magnificent work, just from the sheer amount of material in it. But size and warmth alone were not enough for a marriage quilt, of course. It would have pride of place in the wedding ceremony, showing off that the families coming together had wealth enough to supply that much textile work by artfully draping it over both the hope chests of the new couple, and proudly displaying a stylised family history.

And, of course, proudly displaying an elaborately worked warming spell, to keep the new family safe in the depths of winter. Display was all well and good, but no one *ever* forgot winter this far north.

"Here we are! It's the Donalds and the Montgomerys, Sara and Toby, and I'm having trouble enough finding ways to make the histories of each distinct when they've both been farming practically the same land, so you're going to have your work cut out for you finding a place for all your spell bits."

"Spell*grams*, sister mine, and aye, I can see *that's* going to be a right pickle. Ley-ley, what do you think?"

Leyla was running a careful finger up and down the fabric, seeing the few empty spaces left. "I don't know, Mama. I've never understood why we don't put the spell on the *inside* of the quilt—it should be a lot better protected that way, and there'd be a lot more room."

Hannah grimaced. "Apprentice Leyla, I thought I'd taught you better than that. Aye, the spellwork would last longer, for sure, but how would anyone *check* it on the inside? All it'd take is one thing going wrong and they might roast in their bed. On the outside, it's a lot easier to see if something's off."

"I *guess*, it just seems… *Anyway*, I think we can put the warming spellgram here, and the linking spellgram there, and *either* the limiter or temperature checker here, but I don't know where we can fit the other one."

Hannah nodded, eyes growing abstracted as she started being swept up by the problem. "Aye, yes, I see all that… You couldn't have left this nice space here for us, Rosie?"

Her sister sniffed. "Of course not, don't be silly. Where *else* could I have fit the great *tree* old Joseph *insisted* be there, despite the fact that they sold the last of the orchard to the Martins two generations ago?"

"Aye, that does sound like him all right… Well, let's see what we can do."

Hannah and Leyla got to work, trying out every odd configuration they could think of to make the spell fit. Sometimes they would even succeed, only to be vetoed by Rosie's aesthetic sensibilities, which led to a fair amount of good-natured ribbing from both sides.

"Oh, of *course* I could fit the spell in there! If I were willing to have a *lopsided quilt* on display at the wedding. Sara's a darling—I would *never* do that to her—and Toby's close enough to being good enough for her that I wouldn't wish a bad omen on their marriage."

"Like anyone would notice! It's one *tiny* line of spellwork on one side that isn't on the other, you couldn't even tell more than three feet away!"

"*I* would know, and that's enough, thank you *kindly*, sister-dear."

Hannah returned to muttering and eyeballing, and Leyla recognised that she wouldn't be needed for a bit. She scooched up next to her aunt instead, enjoying watching the embroidery. Each design had been carefully sketched onto heavy paper by one of the embroiders with a good eye, before being pricked through by thorough apprentices, leaving tiny holes matching the design.

Rosie had a stack of these, all standard designs that they re-used regularly, and she would choose one (a stylised mother figure, in this case) to pin to the quilt, before covering the design in a dark powder.

"What's that called, Aunt Rosie?"

"Pounce powder, little Ley, and this is the pounce tool. See how it has a little bit of felt on each side? I'm going to use the dark end for the dark powder, and we force it through the holes…and there, you see?"

She unpinned and carefully lifted the paper straight up, leaving dark dots in the shape of the design behind. "Now, I can follow the pattern with my stitches. *Some* people have to draw in the entire shape to make sure they don't get lost, but I find my way on the points alone."

She raised her voice for this last sentence, and a few rude words floated back from the rest of the circle, making her grin and Leyla giggle.

"Hm…"

"Oh, I recognise *that* 'hm'; I better go check on Mama. Thank you Aunt Rosie!"

"Ah, yes, *that* 'hm'; off you go Leyla."

Hannah's eyes refocused, and she motioned at her daughter. "Octagonal! We can do the limiter in an octagonal pattern!"

"Ye-es, Wizard Hannah, but only if we have a *lot* of space. We have the *opposite* of a lot of space, here, so I don't see how that will help."

Her mother grinned at the overly patient tone, and traced a long line across the edge of the quilt. "Oh, we have *plenty* of space... We'll just run it around the whole thing!"

Leyla scrunched her face up. "Um, Wizard Hannah, I think you need to explain a little better. Aunt Rosie's face is scrunched too, so she's not seeing it either."

"My face is *disbelieving*, not *scrunched*, but yes, I have no idea what you are on about, Hanners."

Hannah waved aside the old nickname. "The octagon doesn't have to be thick, just *long* enough that the corners make the right shape when we turn. We can do it all along the outside edges, here and here, and then follow the path you already have dividing the designs diagonally. It won't be unbalanced, it'll be *even more* balanced!"

Rosie gave her own "Hm," and Leyla traced the proposed path. "Then the temperature checker here, the warmer there, the linker *there*...I think that would work, Aunt Rosie."

"Yes, I do think it would... Very well, you know where the pricker cards are. Chalk it out and let's see what it looks like."

Finding the right papers ended up being the most difficult part, which was resolved when another member of the circle eventually realised what they were looking for and sheepishly handed them over from her worktable. After that, forcing the chalk through and getting a rough idea of the design was simple enough, and Rosie nodded her satisfaction.

"That will do. I assume you're staying for lunch?"
"Of course!"

They settled in for the midday meal, and as Hannah sliced their pie, she held it up for Leyla to see. "What did I tell you? Beef and *fancy* gravy."

The whole circle made them feel welcome, and even without the special pie it would have been a good time. Rosie regaled everyone with a tale from their adolescence that seemed scandalously impossible, except for how much it flustered Hannah. She retaliated in turn by conspiring with the apprentices handing out the food to introduce a bit of soap into Rosie's bread. The outrage in her eyes as she spluttered sent a wave of laughter around the circle.

"Just thought you ought to have your mouth washed out from all that!"

"What, just because *I* learned to speak properly while you still insist on talking like a hayseed? Leyla, at *least* tell me your *father* has been teaching you—"

Some time (and stories) later, Hannah and Leyla started off back home, enjoying the afternoon sun. "It's *always* fun visiting Aunt Rosie."

"Aye, that it is. Be nice if we were a tad closer, but Berrywoods is a little too isolated. We get a lot more business from Bywater than we would out here. Besides, Skye Law wouldn't be at all happy with me trying to poach, and neither of us would do well then."

They continued along for a bit before Leyla asked, "Mama? Why *is* it that you talk differently than Aunt Rosie and Papa?"

Hannah gave a half-grin. "Well…it is not that I *cannot* speak properly if I want to. I can be quite the wordsmith if I so choose."

The change in her speech was so stark that Leyla just stared a moment, tripping and nearly falling over a rut.

Hannah steadied her before reverting back to her normal speech.

"It was those Guild types, down in Meldrum. When... when I went for the examinations, they said a whole lot about villagers who weren't properly educated trying to be better than they ought to be. I decided to make a point of talking like most everyone else around here, before trouncing more than half of them in both the written *and* the practicals. After that..."

She shrugged. "Not much point in talking otherwise, with most of the people we deal with. And...I guess I still wanted to make that point, and then it just became a habit."

They walked on, the silence more melancholy this time. "Mama? What would have happened? If...if you had joined the Guild? You wouldn't have met Papa, would you?"

"I might have, Night-star. But you know your Papa, he doesn't like towns, and as it turns out I don't care for them much either. We're both happier, this way. It's just...it's not the 'might-have-been's that bother me, it's just that it wasn't *my* choice. When they named the joining price, three times what it normally was, just because I'd wounded their pride..."

She shook her head. "That bit still hurts, aye. But they were doing me a favour, in the end. I got your father, and I got you, and our snug little house and visits to your aunt Rosie and all. Speaking of..."

Ciaran opened up the door as they made their way up the walk. "Well, home early! I'm glad the quilt wasn't too troublesome. How was the pie?"

His "innocent" voice fooled no one. "It was lovely, and everyone was jealous. Just like you intended, you transparent bear of a man."

Her husband's grin broadened, and he took the empty basket and their packs. "It's the simple things in life I treasure. I want to hear *all* about it, but first—"

He kissed Leyla's head, and nuzzled his wife.

"Welcome home."

Interlude: Shepshame Festival

Ciaran poured out a pitcher of water to douse the very last embers, the fire having not been fed for some time in preparation for this, and nodded satisfaction. "That does it, the last flame in the house has been extinguished. Ley-ley, if you could just scoop out the remnants there..."

After she had cleared the way, he took the opportunity to give a thorough scrubbing to his beloved oven before laying out the wood for later. While he scrubbed, Leyla went back to helping her mother clean and pack charcoal, feast-ware, a special bottle of drink, blankets, and everything else they might need for the festival. "Right, we've got all four cups, that's the last of it. Good work, Leyla, you can go get dressed now."

As her daughter scampered off to get her festival clothes on (her father having succeeded, with some effort, in convincing her *not* to wear her nice new clothes every day),

Hannah made her own final preparations. Or started to, only to be interrupted by a pair of arms wrapping around her.

"Have I mentioned lately how *very* much I love the cleaning spell you made for me?"

Her smug smile was audible as she leaned back against Ciaran. "Oh, once or twice, but you could tell me again…"

He turned his hands in front of her. "Look! I've been scrubbing for the last hour and you would never know these hands were even *inside* the oven. I'm just glad the Blackhills miners were willing to share that little secret, and every other baker in Bywater agrees."

She captured one of the hands and kissed each finger. "And I can speak for the *spouses* of every baker, it's been a right delight. I suppose it is a *little* extravagant, though…"

"Nonsense—the amount of time I would have to scrub to feel clean enough to cook again would cost *well* more than the little bit of wood it takes to power the spell."

He grinned over his shoulder as he went to put his own festival garb on. "You just focus on the magic and leave the budgeting to me, Hannahlan."

She enjoyed the view for a few moments before an impatient eleven-year-old urged her back into her own preparations. Soon enough, the whole family was walking out in the late afternoon sun, laden with packs and baskets. As they made the main path to the festival grounds, they spotted the Martins ahead, and sped up enough to catch them. "Lachlan, Calvin, good to see you! And Annabelle, you're taller every time I see you!"

Ciaran's brother and his family slowed as they caught up, and Annabelle frowned up at Hannah. "Aunt Hannah, you say that *every time* you see me."

Hannah grinned at the proper little six-year-old in front of her. "It's true! I can't help it if you keep growing. It's your papa and your father you have to talk to about that."

Annabelle looked pensive at this for a moment, before replying, "Okay, I can do that. But still, you should notice other things about me, not just how tall I am. I have a pretty ribbon in my hair, you can notice that."

She pointed at the ribbon in question, and Hannah returned amiably, "And an excellent shade of blue it is!"

Her niece nodded firmly before asking her uncle Ciaran what he had baked for today, and Hannah was able to turn her attention to her brothers-in-law. Lachlan was talking animatedly with Leyla about the latest developments on the orchard. Leyla had felt proprietary about the orchard since warding the cherry trees had been her first task as an apprentice, and Lachlan never needed an excuse to talk about his work.

"Well, Calvin, I see you haven't bashed Lachlan's head in yet, so I take it things are going well?"

The slender man grinned back at the old joke. "Well, not for want of trying, but he never holds still long enough for me to aim! And I see you haven't lit Ciaran's hair on fire recently, so I suppose things are just as well over there."

Hannah laughed. "That was one time! One! You're never going to let me live that down, are you?"

The two families settled into comfortable conversation for the rest of the walk, as they and the rest of the village gathered. Unlike the big Summer Fair, this was mainly a Bywater event (though some with ties from other villages always joined) so the grounds weren't nearly as crowded as they approached. Though, Hannah considered as she craned her head around, they were more crowded every year. She wouldn't be surprised if Bywater was the nearest village for a good thousand people at this point, though she knew the number that paid obligations to (and could in turn expect support from) the village proper was only half, maybe two thirds of that.

Hannah handed off her baskets to Ciaran and Leyla when they reached the bonfire-to-be, and strode off to let them help with various food preparation and whatever else it was they did. *She* had the most important duty today, and nodded greetings to the various loggers and others helping arrange the great pit.

"Hallo, Wizard Hannah, no apprentice today?"

"Sadly not, Collier Liam, her father needed the help more. Something to do with warding the bugs and such away from the feast, as I understand it."

"Ah, good, then we'll see her later at least. Well, as you see, the crew's got most of this well in hand, and young Angus is ready to help you draw everything out for the big event."

Angus ducked his head, still shy around her from the awful events the year before. Hannah would have preferred that he'd gotten over it by now, but on the other hand that might help him avoid another bad mistake in the future, so it was really six the one, half dozen the other. "Right, come along then Angus."

They first walked slow circles around the area, making sure there weren't any rocks or other obstructions that would interfere with the spellscript. There shouldn't be, they used this area every year, but it was always worth checking. Next, they put the markers up on the boundary stones, warning everyone older than the age of six or so not to go inside a spell, and everyone with little ones to make sure they didn't come *near* the area.

Next was double-checking the stencils, and then the drawing itself. They then checked it once independently, and once both together to make sure there was no flaw, and then covered the dirt with a length of canvas. They'd check it again, of course, before actually using the spell, but it was big enough to be worth doing ahead of time.

"Right, I think that's that. Back to filling that pit, Angus, and give the rest of the crew my greetings."

He ducked his head again and nearly ran off. Hannah just shook her head and made her way back to find her family. She was nearly there when the cheer went up, and the lanky wizard turned with a grin to see the first of the shepherds cresting the hill.

"Mama! Papa sent me over to keep an eye on you; *he* says it's a madhouse and he didn't want you getting lost."

Hannah raised an eyebrow at her daughter. "Is that what he said, now?"

"We-*ell*, he *actually* said he didn't want you *pretending* to get lost so you didn't have to help with the food and things, but *I* think my way was politer."

Her mother sighed. "It would have been, if it wasn't so obvious. But thank you for trying, anyhow. Let's get to it, then. At least we can have some nibbles while we work."

"Ooh, good point Mama! I know it's bad luck to eat before the shepherds arrive, but it was really hard waiting…"

If you asked Hannah, the rest of the preparations dragged on for hours. Ciaran likely would have said it was a mere half hour, and Leyla kept getting distracted with each new thing. The sun, while silent on the matter, wordlessly suggested it had been not quite an hour before the cheer went up again as the whole village settled down for the evening meal.

Like most families they had an extra place set, trencher and cup both ready. Every dish that was handed around had at least a little morsel placed on the trencher, and every pitcher granted at least a few drops to the cup. The laughing and singing continued all the while, but each time Hannah added something for the extra place, she took a moment to remember and be thankful for their time together.

Only a moment, though, before she rejoined the merriment.

"The lamb went out, the lamb went down, and the lamb went rollicking on

But the shepherd's eye swept o'er the downs, by hook and crook she searched

'Til at last she came upon the lamb, and found it right at dawn

O she found it right at dawn!"

Eventually, old Finlay stood with the setting sun behind him, and the raucous crowds quieted as his famous glare (and even more famous dogs) brought order to the feast as easily as they corralled a flock.

"Well, now, I've been asked to speak this year, despite thinking this whole thing is a pack of silliness distracting from real work. So I'll make it quick:

"Sky above, earth below, water around and fire within, we give thanks once again for healthy sheep, home once again from the summer pastures. We remember those who are not here with us, and give thanks for the time we had with them. And we give thanks for the fire that keeps us through the winter, and we honour that fire today!"

With that, everyone nodded and responded, "We honour that fire today!" Hannah rose, Ciaran and Leyla carefully handing up the full trencher and filled cup to her as she made her way towards the bonfire. Lennox Milligan ended up next to her, carefully balancing two trenchers and cups as the bonfire was slowly surrounded by untouched food and drink. Lennox returned to stand with his family as Hannah made her way to the spellwork.

She removed the canvas, checked it once, checked it twice, before nodding and taking Ciaran's hand. He in turn held Leyla's, who held Annabelle's, who held Calvin's, who held Lachlan's, and so on all the way around in an ever-growing spiral. And right as the last sliver of sun dipped beneath the hill, Hannah called out, "Fire within, we honour you today!" and stepped into the activation circle.

She and everyone else in that great spiral, designed to draw from each participant equally, felt a sudden weariness as the food and drink they had placed around the pit flared. A great ball of fire began at the far end of the spiral, flying overhead as it traced their pattern, before flinging itself into the pit and lighting the bonfire in a sudden blaze. As was tradition, everyone not mourning a loss shouted their own (often ribald) welcome to shepherds and sheep in a dizzying cacophony. Which allowed each mourner to privately say a few words.

"Aoife, Aunt and Wizard, I wish you could see your grand-niece. I wish you were here to help me guide her. And

I hope you're proud of what the starveling apprentice you took on has become."

She stood then, looking into the fire, before nodding and turning to her family who wrapped her in an immediate embrace. They held each other for a long moment before Hannah broke their private silence. "Well, now. I think it's time we went bobbing for apples, hm? Last one there has to fetch the hazelnuts!"

The rest of the evening was reserved for fun, aside from the poor unfortunates among the shepherds who had drawn the lot to watch the gathered flocks this year, and even then a steady stream of people went to bring them food and drink and keep them company. Hazelnuts were roasted everywhere a firepit was dug, with mild gambling over which nuts would stay and which would fly a common pastime.

Adolescents played a different game with them, naming pairs of hazelnuts after supposed sweethearts, and seeing which pairs stayed together and which flew apart. By tradition, any couple formed during Shepshame with a steady pair of hazelnuts was under a good omen, and there were plenty who wandered away from the firelight to put that to the test.

Each of those firepits was lit from the main bonfire, and whenever people left the festival they lit a torch or lamp to bring that fire back with them to re-light their homes, left dark and cold as part of the ritual.

But, mostly, there was singing. They sang of the approaching winter, and of the wool they used to defy it. They sang of the pastures, and the hills, and the river winding through them.

And they sang of happy memories with those gone by, in the hopes that those who had passed would hear the song and come enjoy the food and drink set aside for them. And if there were wet cheeks during those songs, what of it? Everyone had been bobbing for apples, after all.

Hannah sat on her blanket, drinking it all in, crunching on sweet roasted apple and dark roasted hazelnuts. Ciaran was lending his deep voice to an old sheepcounting song contest, where at the end of each verse they all took a drink, and they lost when the singers couldn't agree on which verse they were on. Leyla had a crowd of *scrupulously* clean children who she deigned to allow play with her cards, the firelight making the art on them seem even more fantastical.

And for a moment, just a moment, the dancing flames seemed to form Aoife's face in a deep smile. Hannah stared until the smoke made her blink, and the moment was gone.

But not forgotten.

Steddles and Stockpiles

Hannah took a bite out of her strip of mutton and leaned back in satisfaction. "Mmm. I'll say this for the salt shortage, fresh meat's a lot cheaper that it would be otherwise. Haven't had meat this many days in a row since..."

She paused, thinking.

"Well, ever, now that I think about it. So enjoy it, Leyley, odds are good you'll be a woman grown and then some before you see this much again."

Leyla grinned. "Oh, I'm enjoying it, Mama! Almost two weeks in a row of mutton and beef and pork, and Papa getting to try out all *kinds* of things he normally doesn't get to do except for special occasions? And I've got my cards, and my pretty cloak, and everything else, it's been the best year of my life!"

Hannah grinned back, though a trifle uneasily. It was all well and good until *next* year seemed a let-down... Well, perhaps she wasn't giving Leyla enough credit. Planting season had been hard, and she'd borne up under that strain better than her mother had expected. She finished the last of her breakfast, and gathered everything up.

"Well, let's see what we can do to help store everything else. Won't be near as much meat 'til next slaughter season, so we'll need more of all the rest."

They walked out into the crisp autumn morning, hot food in their bellies and warm cloaks on their shoulders making it reasonably pleasant rather than a burden. The leaves swirled around with the wind, showing the usually invisible currents and eddies of the sky to all who cared to see, and they enjoyed mapping the air as they walked.

Their first stop was nearby, and Hannah wanted to cover a few things before they arrived, so she reluctantly cut short their discussion. "Now, Apprentice Leyla, what're the three biggest things everyone worries about when storing foodstuffs?"

"Keeping things dry, or wet; keeping them the right temperature, usually cool; and keeping vermin out!"

"Good! Now, we're mostly going to be double-checking or renewing existing spells over the next week or so, but we should always keep our eyes open for any opportunity to *improve* the spellwork in a storehouse. Won't happen often—everyone knows what they need pretty well—but even once or twice a season where we can make a difference adds up."

Leyla nodded. "Yes, Wizard Hannah, especially since it's multilp—, multpli—" She paused and marshalled her mouth: "*Multiplicative.* A little bit that spoils makes a lot spoiled, but if we can keep the little bit from happening, we can save the lot from happening too."

Hannah grinned. "Ah, you *have* been reading those circulars I set you, then. Aye, that's right, though normally we just say that an ounce of prevention's worth a pound of cure."

Leyla's eyes widened. "Oh, *that's* what that means!"

Her mother paused, re-evaluating her next words. "…What did you think it meant?"

"I thought those were names for herbs. Like…cedar and tansy. Cedar prevents moths, but it's *so* expensive, and tansy cures all kinds of things but it's easy to find."

Hannah pondered that for a moment. "I can see that, aye. But no, it's generally the other way around. Stopping something from happening is usually easier and you're better off doing that than waiting to fix it after something's gone wrong."

Leyla considered that. "Hm! I suppose that makes sense, though I think there's *lots* of things that are easier to fix than stop happening… But not with food storage, I suppose…"

"Well, you learn something new every day. And here's our first stop, so just in time."

The first storehouse of the day stood before them, a small granary where several families stored their harvest. Like many storehouses and other buildings that needed to be out of the damp and kept away from pests, it was raised off the ground by short pillars of stone capped with stone heads, looking for all the world like stone mushrooms that had chosen to grow up under a building. The largest granaries would sit on sixteen of these steddle stones, but this was only a nine-steddle granary.

First they went to examine the stones, which were kept free of lichen and anything else that might make them easier to climb. All nine were inscribed with vermin wards, cleverly powered by any critter that touched them, to keep anything tenacious enough to try and climb up not just the stone cylinders but the overhanging caps from succeeding. Ciaran had told her the families had been complaining about rats still managing to get in somehow, and Hannah had a suspicion about what might be causing that.

"All right, Apprentice, all the outer stones seem to be in good working order. Go check the middle one and see if there's anything wrong with it."

She held Leyla's cloak as the eleven-year-old made her way carefully under the building. "Wizard Hannah, you were right, they haven't been cleaning this regularly, there's all *kinds* of stuff growing on it. I can't tell if there's a hole, but this has *got* to be where they are coming in."

"Thought so. Out of sight and out of mind, it's one of the most common problems. Come on out, we'll just let them know they need to *keep* it in mind. Once they've had a chance to clean it up right, we can swing by again and check the spellwork… If they want to pay for the time. We'll see what they tell your father, but my guess is they'll feel right sheepish, give whichever of 'em was in charge of steddle cleaning a good talking-to, and that'll be that."

Leyla scrambled back out, and they went on to the next place on their rounds.

"Now, Edith Mullen was telling your father that the rot-warner in her root cellar kept going off, but she couldn't find anything wrong. One time, it even went off when there wasn't anything *in* the cellar, so something's not right. When we get there, I want you to look it over without me, first, see what you can tell."

"Um…yes, Wizard Hannah."

"You read up on the rot-warners like I told you to, aye?"

Leyla gulped at the edge in her mother's voice. "I… *almost* finished them…but Mister Robertson was coming out for his hunting, and I only had a little bit of time left to spend in the treehouse…"

Hannah's face was grim. "Oh, so *that's* how it was. Well, let's see if you read enough to find the problem. You do, and it'll *just* be some extra chores with your father and some extra circulars. If you don't find the issue, then I'll have to think about whether you should be spending time in that treehouse for a season or two."

Leyla made a small noise, and kept her head down as they descended into the root cellar. Hannah kept her stony expression while she worried if that had been too harsh, or not harsh enough. Her daughter had at least *strongly* implied that she'd finished all her circulars the other day, though she'd have to check with Ciaran if he could remember the exact words used. But nearly lying and lying outright weren't that far apart, especially on something important like their wizard work. If even one spell they worked on didn't work as promised, that could undo years spent building a reputation that could compete with the Guild.

The young apprentice quietly began examining the rot-warner spell, carefully comparing it to the stencil Edith had left out for them. She frowned at one point, checked something again, and then traced the lines of one section with her finger before getting up and going to examine the door.

"Wizard Hannah? I think…I'm pretty sure…I don't think the spell is pointed correctly. It looks like it's adapted from an older spell for an *attached* root cellar, and it's boundaries are set both on distance and based off how thick the earth or wood or anything else is around it. But this door is pretty thin, and it's close enough to the spell that distance wouldn't stop it."

She fidgeted a moment. "May I go find something that would set it off? I'd like to put something wrong in front of the door a bit, and see if that triggers the spell."

Hannah nodded, and Leyla left, carefully closing the door behind her. Soon enough, she heard footsteps outside, and then thumping as the rot-warner drum began beating. *Tum-tum-tum-tum*, then a long pause, then another *tum-tum-tum-tum*. Hannah shivered a bit as she went to open the door. Root cellars were dark places, and that drum was a *little* too much like a heartbeat for her.

"That did it—good spotting. I guess you really must have been paying attention, at least to what you read. We'll settle the rest of *that* later, but for now, good work. We'll let Butcher Edith know, and see if she wants us to fix it or handle it herself."

The tension in her daughter's shoulders relaxed as she breathed out a relieved sigh. "Thank you, Wizard Hannah."

The rest of the day, and the next several days, followed a similar pattern. Granaries and root cellars weren't the only places they visited, however, and larders, springhouses, hay lofts, even beehives on their own individual steddle stones, all saw attention from the wizard and her apprentice. Not to mention plenty of enjoyment of the fallen leaves swirling in the wind, pine needles crunching underfoot, ripe apples, and fluffy sheep and goats growing out their winter coats.

Near the end of their rounds, however, Hannah finally spotted something more interesting. "Well, now, what have we here?"

They were in a springhouse, the spring itself running through riverstone-lined channels back and forth to provide as much cooling as possible to the pans of milk and other dairy goods stored there. They were inspecting vermin wards, which all seemed in order.

"Ley-ley…didn't your father say Milker Casey told him that they were having an issue with some of his milk not clabbering the right way, and just getting nasty?"

"Yes, Mama. I think he said it was just some parts of it, and just sometimes, but he thought maybe something was getting in past the wards to, um, piddle in it or something like that. He also said it looked and tasted different even before it went nasty."

Hannah grinned. "I think I know what's wrong. Come look at this."

Leyla scooched over, curious.

"Now, here's some milk, right? Looks like milk, tastes like milk…" She dipped a finger in and licked it. "It's milk. Now, watch this…"

The wizard dipped a small ladle into the milk, and poured a dollop onto the vermin wards. They both watched, and Leyla hesitantly stuck her own finger out and tasted the milk still left in the ladle, and then the milk on the wards.

"The ward did something to the milk? It tastes different…it even looks a little different, though not much. But… why would the ward do anything to the milk?"

"Well, now, I'm not sure about the *why*, but it definitely *is*. And I think I know when it started—look."

She took the little ladle again, and tilted it so a tiny dribble came over the side and touched the warded area. Now that they were both watching, they could see the milk change colour, even inside the ladle.

"Ohhh… If even a little bit touches, but *that* bit is touching the rest…"

"The wards kill…whatever it is they're killing, and that changes the milk. They wouldn't have had that problem before; they only switched to killing wards last season after some persistent critter kept breaking through the old wards and they wanted to send a message. And that's fine, and all, as long as they don't let the milk spill."

Hannah raised a finger. "But, we could certainly modify the wards so they didn't do that to the milk, though we'd have to test a bit to figure out how. And either way, now we know what's going on, which will make Milker Casey happy."

Leyla nodded. "Who would have thought there was something *alive* in *milk*? I don't know how he would have ever thought of that."

Hannah stood, wincing a little as she realised she'd been kneeling on hard ground for longer than she should have. "Aye, I sure wouldn't have. And I'm glad that's sorted; I like the baking they do with that clabbered milk too much to be happy about anything interrupting it. Let's go let him know."

After a brief discussion, which didn't surprise Casey as much as they had thought it would, they went on their way. Eva Nelson gave them a pot of butter to take back with them, asking them to tell Ciaran this was the butter/herb mix he had asked about, and they happily agreed.

The walk home through the late afternoon was restful. The shorter days meant neither were as tired as they had been in other seasons, and they were looking forward to another luxurious meal with meat and new butter for their bread.

Ciaran welcomed them as usual as Leyla excitedly began to tell him about their day. Hannah waited her turn with her husband as he smiled at the bouncing girl.

"And *then* we found out that it was the *wards* that were the problem, because the milk is *alive*, or, well, something *in* the milk is alive, we're not exactly sure and Mama and I were going back and forth on that, and Milker Casey wasn't surprised but *I* was surprised, were you surprised Papa?"

"I can't say I'm *too* surprised, though I wouldn't have guessed it. Milk does all kinds of things, it makes sense that it's still alive, in a way. Now I see that you have the butter Eva was telling me about, and we have a wonderful beef stew, so let's discuss the rest at the table. But, first—"

He squeezed his daughter as he picked her up, making her giggle, and pulled Hannah in for a kiss.

"Welcome home."

Winter's Bite

Hannah sipped her soup slowly, enjoying the heat from the ceramic mug on her hands. She could see her daughter was doing the same, though that might also just have been from a burned tongue as she tried to slurp it in too quickly earlier.

She couldn't fully relax, though, not with the howling wind reminding her what the rest of the day would be like. It would be rough going in some places…

"At least your father was able to clear a bit of a path for us, Ley-ley. Doesn't seem like there's more snow just yet, so we should be able to at least walk instead of forcing our way through, at first."

Leyla grinned up at her. "You did the thing again, Mama. That was a conversation just in your head, not with me."

Hannah rolled her eyes. "Like you couldn't follow it just fine, after all these years."

"Still! Papa asked me to remind you, and you sighed and agreed, and a good wizard always takes a grumbled 'yes' over a shouted 'no.'"

Her mother glared over the top of her steaming mug. "Using my own words against me, now? Why did I bother teaching you again?"

"Because I'm helpful, and smart, and *adorable*."

Hannah couldn't help laughing at the cheerful response. "All right, you win this round. I'll get the beginning part of the conversation out before the middle part, next time."

"And I'll remind you if you don't!"

Leyla nodded firmly, finished the last of her soup, and stood to go dress for the day. Under the circumstances, that was going to be a more involved task than usual, and Hannah sighed, drained her own mug, and went to follow suit.

The plan today was *layers*. They would be in and out of warm spaces, as some of their work was inside and some out, and even a little sweat while they were inside would make them curse their own names when they went back outside. Adding to that scarves, shapeless mittens, ear-covering hats tied down firmly, and their usual packs, Hannah felt like a bear right after fattening season. She nearly knocked a few stencils off the rack as she manoeuvred her way toward the door.

"Fr-ah-oh, who cares, *frost* these mittens! I *hate* feeling like I can't use my fingers. Come on, Ley-ley, and you get one free swear later if you don't tell your father about mine."

Leyla's muffled voice came from just behind her: "Deal, Mama!"

"Off to a great start, bribing my daughter before we're out the door. Hope it's not an omen... Okay, I'm opening the door, come out right after me and I'll close it as quick as can be."

She forced the door open, struggling against the wind, and stepped through as Leyla scampered behind. She had to struggle nearly as much to get the door closed without slamming loudly enough to wake half the village, not to mention her husband, and then took a moment. The howling made it difficult to even hear her own thoughts, and she could feel it trying to claw into every nook and cranny in her garb.

Hannah strode off, not even trying to talk, and did her best to stay upwind of Leyla. It was rough going, but if she could keep the little apprentice in the lee of the wind then she might be able to keep up with the rangy wizard. Or so Hannah hoped, at least.

She blessed Ciaran repeatedly as they walked. The wind had driven plenty of snow back onto the paths, but it was loose and easy enough to walk through. All of the hard-packed (and ice-laminated) snow had been cut through and moved, not just down their walk but a good ways down the lane to the village proper before the usual village crews had clearly taken over. It was *absolutely* worth the massaging (and other thank yous) she had given him the night before, and then some.

The cold was another matter. They had been accumulating more clothing this year, and thankfully much of it after Leyla's last growth spurt, but only some of it was really *designed* for this. She was *very* grateful this had not happened last year, when they had been much less prepared, but that didn't make this pleasant.

As they struggled along, she could see the ice of the river glinting under the snow drifts. That had been the first dire omen, a couple of weeks earlier. Ice *in* the river was common enough, deep in winter, but the entire river freezing was a rare occurrence. The entire river freezing at the *beginning* of winter had only happened once before, that anyone could remember.

They finally made it in to the long, low building of their destination, and after a struggle made it inside and relatched the door. They immediately began peeling layers down, and the stark difference in heat felt oppressive until they finished. Leyla's face was red, and she leaned against the door for a moment, just breathing. Hannah couldn't blame her, and just hoped they could avoid any kind of illness from the wide swings in heat and cold.

"I'm right glad you could make it, Wizard Hannah, 'Prentice Leyla. I know things are bad out today, but it doesn't seem like they'll be getting any better, either."

Hannah puffed out a breath. "Aye, that it doesn't, Swineherd Harriet. All the more reason to get this sorted now. As I understand it, you're worried about temperature swings from the mucking out?"

Harriet nodded. "Normally, it's not much of an issue—they keep themselves clean and know where to do their business, but if we let them out in this cold we've seen them get mighty ill from going out and in, not to mention how much heat we lose in the house. But if they stay in, we still have to open up and the pens closest the door are getting cold enough to be trouble. We're doing what we can with blankets and such, but…" She shrugged. "We don't keep *that* many, over winter, and it'll likely be less if this keeps up. Feed'll be too dear. So I can't afford to lose any to illness, if I can help it."

Hannah rubbed her lips. "I think I have something that'll help with that. We'll get to work, and we can talk efficiencies and such once we've tested."

Harriet nodded back worriedly and returned to chopping wood, leaving Hannah and Leyla and the swine.

"Now, Apprentice Leyla, I've been pondering something like this for a bit... I think we might be able to use something like the anvil spell."

Leyla's face crinkled. "Wouldn't that make things *way* too hot, Wizard Hannah?"

"It doesn't have to be *that* hot. It's just the trick of making it maintain an even temperature. We just want the pens to be warm enough, all the time. It'll only burn fuel when it gets too cold, like a frost ward, but this should work on the air in the pens well enough."

Leyla nodded slowly. "I think I see how that would work... I'll get everything set up."

In the end, it took some trial and error, but they were able to do something with the temperature sensing from the anvil spell, the sudden start from a frost ward, and a variant on a wedding quilt spell to take into account the heavy blankets and other nesting material to make sure the pigs didn't end up overheated. It was complicated, and had to be adjusted for every pen, but ended up being surprisingly efficient. Harriet was overjoyed, and Hannah was smiling as they began layering up for the next trek.

"Now, remember, there's a bit of a pickle that can happen if you use linen blankets instead of wool. It's too much to be worth going into, but just stick with wool blankets and you'll be fine. Linen ones might get them overheated, and burn way more fuel than needed."

"Easy enough to remember, and I appreciate you, Wizards! May Sky Above take some pity on you and have the wind bite a little less as you walk."

"From your lips to the winds themselves, Swineherd Harriet."

The rest of the day was similar. They walked, leaning into the wind, through the village and farms and pastures. They worked on spells of heat, as well as renewing charms to prevent axes from slipping and feet from skidding. And everywhere they went, they saw the worry.

Food wasn't the problem, although it would be a bland season. There was plenty in the granaries, and more than a few blessed the foresight that had led to the village investing in a few sixteen-steddle granaries with preservation spells a few years back. So there was little danger of anyone in Bywater starving, though everyone knew village obligations would be higher the next year, to make up for using the stores.

It wasn't the snow, either. There *was* snow, and would likely be more, but not so much that roofs were in danger of collapsing. It was yet another burden in a season that seemed likely to be filled with them, but not a danger in itself.

It was the cold.

Animals brought in for the season were as welcome for the body heat they added to homes as the meat and everything else they promised for the future. Everyone who could was gathering and chopping wood, and the logging teams were working every hour of daylight, and discussing using light spells to keep going after dark, despite the risks. Blackhills sent word that they were switching to mining veins of heating coal, instead of coking coal, and Bywater's Council set aside over half the village coin reserves to buy whatever they could get from the miners.

Children were stuffing rags between shutters, trying to eke out any bit of extra insulation they could. The hunters and trappers were already muttering that a winter like this would lead to wolves starving, maybe enough for them to risk attacking people, and traps and wolf-killing spells were being prepared.

Around midday, they were helping Quinn alter her usual smithy spells to handle being closed in, as even the blacksmith did not wish to work exposed to the elements now, when a particularly fierce howl made the smith shake her head.

"As bad as winter's going to be, I can't say I'm looking forward to spring. You know what they say, the flood's often worse than the frost." She waved a finger over at the snickering Leyla. "Those were perfectly accurate descriptions, not swears, so don't you go taking that as license."

Leyla started to agree, paused, and then gave the older woman a wicked grin. "Of course not, Chiefsmith! But Mama *did* say I got one free swear, so…"

She inhaled, and Hannah flushed as Quinn raised an eyebrow at the wizard.

"*FLOOD IT!*"

Hannah hid her face in her hands, as Quinn started cackling, and one of her strikers came to investigate the shout. Quinn managed a wave to show him it was all right, and he just shook his head at the tableau before returning to his own work. Hannah could *feel* the grin coming from her daughter, and just sighed.

"Hannah, if that's your daughter's idea of 'naughty,' then you're doing just fine as a parent, trust me. The trouble that your aunt got into when she was that age…hm. That reminds me…"

Hannah risked removing her face from her hands, though she steadfastly did *not* look in her daughter's direction.

"Do you remember the story Aoife had from *her* grandmother, about that wild-flood that swept through in her day?"

"Aye, it was a staple anytime someone complained about a bad flood. 'Back before your grandparents were born, we had *real* flooding! Whole trees, boulders, ice, all packed together, sweeping down the river, destroying *everything in its path*!'"

Quinn grinned. "I always did enjoy her pretending to be an old codger. I remember one winter the two of you were working on a spell to deal with a wild-flood, if another ever came."

She nodded towards the distant mountains. "I've never seen the river freeze this early. If it's that bad in the mountains… Might be we'll need something to deal with another wild-flood."

Hannah gave a low whistle. "You think? I've tinkered on it, with Ciaran and then Leyla, just for idle fun, but…you're right, couldn't hurt, might help. Would need an awful lot of power, though."

Quinn shrugged. "Only if it's used. You'd just need enough burnables by the river, somewhere, and if it never happened then they'd go right back where they came from."

"Hm. All right, Auntie Quinn, I'll work on it."

Late in the short winter day they were at Rae and Tristan Milligan's house again, working on spells to help the pair cut through the ice and continue fishing. When they finished coming up with a different application from the anvil spell to heat specific segments of ice to make it easier to chisel through, Hannah was surprised to see Tristan with a full basket of fish for her at the door. He had clearly taken advantage of Leyla packing in the next room to steal a word with Hannah, and she was initially wary.

"Fisher, you know that it's Ciaran you settle up with, what's all this?"

Tristan handed it over, wrapping her mittened-hand around the handle. "And I'll do that with him. This is for something else."

The eyes of the normally fidgety (Hannah might even have said "flighty") man were focused and intent, almost hot. "This is for the name on our house. We've been able to keep little Evie comfortable, and Rae's been able to *rest* and take care of her because we haven't had to worry about enough fuel for the bin, because of you."

"Your father-in-law paid for that—"

"But no one else could have done it. The Guild Wizards in Meldrum won't even take commissions for naming, even the University ones are wary. He paid for it, and I'm grateful to him, for sure and certain, but *you* did it."

His voice was firm, and brooked no argument. "We'll never know how it would have gone, otherwise, but as far as I'm concerned, you saved my daughter, and kept my wife from killing herself trying to work when she should rest. This fish is just a token, and if there's ever anything we can do to repay you, just say the word."

Hannah met his eyes, and nodded slowly. "Aye, Tristan Milligan, I will. But here's the first part of it. I know Foreman Lennox did wrong by Rae, he knows it too. But he's trying, and he's just as responsible for this as I am. Talk with Rae, and see if maybe little Evie can help reconcile her mother and grandfather."

Tristan considered this for a moment. "Done. We still owe you, though. Just say the word."

"I will."

He released her, and went to go rejoin his wife and daughter, passing a curious Leyla. Hannah could tell Leyla wanted to ask questions, and for once today she was grateful for the whipping wind as they left the house.

The trek home was hard. They were tired, the wind was colder and stronger, and while the sun had not yet set, the thin light was blocked by threatening clouds as often as not. They were dragging slowly as they trudged up the walk, and rarely had Ciaran's welcome been *so* welcome.

He helped them out of their various layers, and half-carried Leyla to the table. Hannah could smell a strong barley stew, and shivered with anticipation at how good it would feel inside her stomach. Ciaran helped her into a chair, and bustled about putting bread and stew in front of them, along with hot cider.

"I'm glad to have you home. That should handle the last of the work for a few days, and I want *both* of you to just stay home. I'll handle it if the village needs emergency labour."

Hannah nodded gratefully, and Leyla was practically falling asleep in her stew but managed a weak "Thank you, Papa" despite it.

"The rest will do you good. And these walls keep the cold out well—I know everyone with the new double-walled houses was talking them up in the market, me included. There was some talk about working to replace all the old walls, though I doubt the Council will make it a requirement. That would be far too expensive for most, and the obligations we'd have to pay to have the village fund it… I'm just grateful we have one, and a good name to go with it."

Ciaran kissed his wife's knuckles, and wrapped an arm around each of their shoulders. "Now, eat and drink, and I'll tuck both of you into bed. I'll handle everything else."

He squeezed both of them, and Hannah tilted her head onto her husband's broad shoulder, relaxing into his warmth. "You have to say the words, though. I like th'words."

Leyla, arms wrapped around her Papa, nodded vigorously. Ciaran smiled, and kissed both of them.

"Welcome home."

Interlude: Wild-Flood

Hannah finished carving the last rye spell on the plank, and handed it off to Leyla. "That should do it. I'll leave you to put everything back and pack. Come meet me when you're done. The Council meeting should be over, and I want to talk with your father."

Her daughter nodded, and gave her a quick hug. "I'll handle it, Wizard Hannah."

The tall wizard strode as quickly as she dared down the muddy lanes of early spring. The Springsfirst festival had been subdued as everyone took in the damage from the awful winter, but it had been later than usual which meant the planting season was even tighter than usual, too. She had wanted to be *in* the meeting, but there was just too much to be done, and she knew Ciaran was better at convincing people than she was, anyway.

She turned the corner and saw the various councillors going their separate ways, as well as her husband standing.

He spotted her, and shook his head. She winced and slowed down. There wasn't a reason to rush now.

"I'm sorry, Hannah. With the reserves so low already, and so much damage that has to be handled, they were not interested in planning for something that hasn't happened in so long."

She sighed, and rested her head on his chest. "Flood it. I knew that was possible, but it won't even cost hardly anything if it doesn't happen…"

"It's not the cost, love, it's the capital. There are so many things the village needs right now; tying up that much of the resources was just…"

Ciaran trailed off. He knew the reasons why didn't really matter. Ever since Quinn had mentioned it, they had both been asking around and other families had stories of the wild-flood, and everyone agreed conditions seemed to match the stories. Some of the river traders even confirmed that they had seen one a decade or so ago on the other side of Bended Fork. With a little actual *focus*, and another technique derived from the anvil spell, she had been able to get a workable spell together that she thought would deal with the wild-flood…if they could get enough power for it.

Hannah straightened, and took a deep breath. "Well… all right, so we find the burnables another way. How much would that amount of coal or charcoal cost?"

Her husband winced. "Right now? With everyone still recovering from winter? More than we could manage, even with the promise of returning it or selling it later if it wasn't needed."

She nodded grimly. "Then we call in favours. We start *owing* favours, if we need to. I can feel it in my bones, Cirie. I don't think it was an accident, Quinn reminding me. I think

Aunt Aoife nudged her to warn us. It was bad enough all those years ago, that was before the bridge, and all the docks downriver of it, all the *waterwheels* upstream and down… If we lost *all* of that…"

Ciaran looked at her carefully. "It could take us years to pay those kinds of favours back. Long, lean years, just like we were finally out of. Are you *that* certain?"

"Yes."

He nodded. "Then I'll start having conversations. We've built up enough goodwill… But anything you can add will help. Just get them to agree and send them to me to coordinate. I'll handle the details."

There was plenty of gossip around the village over the next couple of months. The wizard and the spellbinder were taking all the barter they accumulated, and turning it into burnables. Everything they could borrow or beg they were doing, which occasioned more than a little mirth among certain sorts, as Hannah had refused to beg for anything since she was a girl. And more than a few rolled their eyes at the silly notion of a "wild-flood" that hadn't been seen in most of a century.

But, quietly, bins were built and filled at a narrow stretch of rapids, upriver of the last waterwheel and most of the farms. And some, though not all, of the gossips took on a more thoughtful tone as they saw how many contributed. Many of the contributions were small, just a few scoops, but those scoops added up. The larger shipments, though, occasioned more talk.

The Berrywoods embroidery circle sending everything they could spare was no surprise. Everyone except Hannah knew Rosie idolised her sister, and since the circle was a sisterhood in more ways than one, they all wanted to help.

Quinn Davis started offering discounts if people paid in burnables and could transport them upriver. And Calvin and Lachlan Martin's "payment in advance" for next year's wizarding work from their sister-in-law, all in charcoal, fooled no one.

Other contributions were more surprising. Liam Bain of the charcoal burners turned in their year's charcoal to the village in late spring, on the condition that it be held in the Hendry bins until it was actually due. That caused a short dispute in the Council, which ended up being settled when Thomas and Angus Buchan came to an open session and made the point that there were plenty of woods near Oak Landing, too, and they didn't *need* to be associated with Bywater.

An entire wagon of coal from Blackhills was purchased by one Trader Lukas Robertson, who asked that the Hendrys store it for him until he could shepherd it downriver personally next autumn. When asked, he cheerfully replied, "Well, now, I'm a trader! I know a good deal when I see one, and getting paid to wait to sell something that I can get just as good a price on later is a fine way to make a little extra coin. And besides, what if she's right? I don't want to lose my favourite hunting grounds just because the docks and bridge are swept away, and I wouldn't want to bet against Hannah, no I would not!"

A few of the wizards from other villages, loosely led by Evan Dawson from Oak Landing, sent a large shipment of charcoal, claiming that they were just getting ready for the Summer Fair, and looking forward to seeing something impressive. "She called lightning from a clear, blue sky. Just *think* how exciting it will be with some more power behind her!"

But the most surprising of all was when Foreman Lennox Milligan addressed the Council on behalf of the quarry, and told them bluntly that the quarry was calling in the debt owed by the village, in its entirety. That caused more than a little panic, as the work to put slate roofs on every home some years ago had been well worth it, to reduce the risk of fire, but they had expected to be paying it back for years yet.

He let them argue and work themselves up for a time, and then just as bluntly told them that the only thing that would change his mind was putting every reserve burnable they had in the new bins upriver. He told them they had a day to decide, and then turned on his heel and walked out. When he returned the next day, the answer was predictable.

Everyone in the village was discussing it. Not because he had been bluntly rude to the Council—that wasn't unusual for the dour foreman. No, the *real* gossip was that after bending the Council to his will, he had marched right down the river and spent an entire day with his daughter's family. And the next market day, he and Rae and Tristan did their shopping together, with him holding little Evie.

And so, at last, Hannah had her power. Begged and borrowed, teetering on the edge of complete financial collapse, but she had it. Ciaran inscribed the spell on a stone in the midst of all the bins, and slate covers protected it. Several of the village children were quietly bribed to keep an eye out for the signs that a wild-flood might be coming. All the preparations, the focus of months of work (on top of all their *usual* work), were finally done.

The waiting nearly drove Hannah (and Ciaran and Leyla) mad, in a way that the worry about preparing in time had not. The Summer Fair was approaching, and word came down that spring was finally reaching even the deepest mountains, and the worry pulsed in the back of her mind like a second heart. If nothing happened by the Fair…

But one day, on a warm, muggy summer day better suited for long afternoon naps than anything else…

"Wizard Hannah! Wizard Hannah the river's running low!"

Her head snapped around, and spotted the girl, one of the Tanners, running pell-mell towards them. She and Leyla were out on their rounds, heading to the dyeworks next. All of that flew out of her mind as she shrugged out of her pack and took off running.

She could see it now, the water was a good foot, no, *two* feet lower than it should have been. Leyla was gathering up her pack and walking stick, but all that was behind Hannah now as she ran, hoping the stories were right about how much time she had.

The water level dropped lower, lower as she sprinted around the bend, and she could hear *something* over the pounding of the blood in her ears.

She reached the spell, gasping, and frantically pulled the slate cover off, readying the activation spellgram.

She could hear it clearly now, cracking and rumbling as the river fell to a trickle.

And then she saw it. A great, shuddering, roiling mass. The glint of ice sparkled amidst the mud and what looked like entire trees, great boulders, and all of it hurtling *at her*. At the corner of this little bend.

She had just a moment to realise that if she failed, they would never find what was left of her, before she touched the spellgram that brought it all to life.

And as the great roaring shook the very ground she stood on, the spell struck. All the bins, coal and charcoal, and every wood pile they could manage flared.

And the wild-flood recoiled from the raw force, as dozens of invisible knives sliced it, carving through it. Dicing it, flinging the chunks backwards into the roiling water behind. Turning one great mass into countless pieces, scattering them across half a mile of water.

And that water hit the bank, right in front of Hannah.

Activating the flood wards, which flared to life and redirected the force downriver. She could hear other wards flaring, as the force of the floodwaters was channelled and dissipated, turning slowly from a raging torrent into…a river.

She heard a shout, and saw Leyla and the Tanner girl running up from behind a hill, whooping and cheering.

"You *did* it, Mama! *You did it!*"

And Hannah, hardly daring to believe it, looked out at the turbulent brown water as her legs shook beneath her.

"*We* did it, Night-star. *We* did it."

She went down with an explosive breath as her daughter tackled her, and her last thought before she focused fully on the double-armful of girl was:

"But what happens *now*?"

Aftermath

As it turned out, what happened next was a lot of discussion. Despite Hannah's spell and all the flood wards, there was still plenty of damage downstream, as chunks of rocks and boulders battered the docks and waterwheels. At first, there was scepticism about how dire the wild-flood had truly been, though that was put to rest as shaken fur trappers, upriver farmers, and other outlying sorts filtered back in to the village with harrowing tales of destruction upstream.

What was left of the burnables had to be redistributed, though the Council fairly promptly assumed responsibility for the various debts, given how much damage had been avoided. The wizards agreed that no one was going to best Hannah, and unanimously declared her the winner of the Summer Fair, saving at least a little grief there.

But one evening, a few weeks later, there was a knock on the door. Ciaran's eyebrows rose as he opened it, and Blair Harper stood with a humourless grin.

"Welcome, Fuller Blair, we weren't expecting—"

She snorted and pushed past him. "Of course you weren't, Spellbinder, and today it's 'Councillor,' thank you."

The older woman set her walking stick aside, and made her way in front of the table where the family had been eating.

"Well, Wizard Hannah, Spellbinder Ciaran, and yes, Apprentice Leyla, you have created more than your share of issues for the Council, and I have been sent to inform you of your punishment."

Ciaran squeezed his daughter's arm warningly, and replied before Hannah could formulate her own response. "Our family has *saved* the Council from considerably more issues than we have created, Councillor."

Her lips pulled back further, baring her teeth more than grinning, now. "Oh, no doubt, but as you will soon learn, young man, few *indeed* remember what you did for them yesterday, only that today you have made their life more difficult. But enough interruptions—I am here to deliver your sentence!"

She pointed, first at Hannah, then at Ciaran.

"You, Wizard Hannah, and you, Spellbinder Ciaran, are *cordially* invited to join the Council. In other words, *you* made this mess, and now *you* get to help clean it up. As always, it is your household that has a seat on the Council, so you get one vote between you, and I personally hope you have many long and fruitless arguments about which way you vote."

Hannah traded looks with Ciaran before cautiously saying, "Our 'punishment' is getting to join the Council? Have a chance to actually make things work better around the village?"

Blair vented a sharp laugh. "Hah! Is *that* what you think we do? Well, you'll learn soon enough. Your first meeting will be two market days from now—we need time for the official announcement and all that drivel. Now, young man, I'm tired and want my own home, no matter how 'cosy' you find yours to be. See me to the door and hand me one of those rolls, and I will be on my way. No, don't fuss, you won't want to be courteous to me after a few Council sessions, and I see no reason to pretend otherwise now."

After the door closed behind her, walking stick in one hand and a fresh roll in the other, Ciaran sat back at the table. "Mama? Papa? Isn't this...*good* news? *Everyone* listens to the Council. Next time there's a wild-flood, or something like that, won't it be easier?"

Ciaran smiled. "It is, yes. Don't let Councillor Blair confuse the matter *too* much. Yes, there is a lot of work to be done, and yes, it won't always be pleasant, but it *matters*."

Hannah twisted her hair around a finger. "Sure didn't sound that way, the way she described it." She couldn't help thinking how much easier it would be to get a Councillor's daughter in to the University than a local village wizard's daughter, though. She pulled more tightly on her hair. It would take years more training, and a lot of saving, but maybe it wasn't so far-fetched a dream after all...

"That's because Blair Harper is a harridan. She is effective and competent, but that doesn't mean we have to accept her interpretation. This is an *honour*. And yes, comes with an extra helping of arguments, but I know how to *negotiate* with the best of them."

Hannah enjoyed the wicked grin on her husband's face.

"I'll let you know when I need you, Hannahlan, but I can handle most of the Council muck. And now, no matter what else might happen, we have a chance to *make things better*."

Both Hannah and Leyla couldn't help smiling at the quiet passion in his voice.

"Now, enough sombre discussion. This calls for a celebration! Lachlan gave something to me years ago, said to save it for the right moment, and I can't think of a better one."

He left the table again, and they could hear him rummaging for a good few minutes before he returned with a small keg.

"This is a special cordial. He normally sells it for *gold* to a factor in Meldrum."

Leyla's eyes widened, and Hannah gave a low whistle. Ciaran bustled about, setting a healthy mug of it in front of each of them.

"I think a toast is in order. Leyla, would you like to start?"

She thought for a moment, before raising her mug. "To always learning more, so we can fix things that need fixing!"

Ciaran smiled and raised his own mug. "To standing on the shoulders of giants. Without Aoife's warning and stories...this would be a much darker season."

They both turned and looked to Hannah, who raised her own mug. "To the future. I don't know what else lies ahead, but I know there's no one else I'd rather see it with."

They clinked their mugs, and drank.

Acknowledgements

The list of people who helped this become a reality is rather daunting to think about, but I want to do justice to as many of them as possible.

First, for the authors who inspired much of this:

Tamora Pierce, for showing me early on that books about the everyday of fantastical settings could be even more fascinating than the fight against the next Dark Lord.

J.R.R Tolkien, for all the many obvious reasons, but particularly for showing a young boy that he did not need to be bound by the time he was born to.

Lois McMaster Bujold, for being quite simply the most wonderful author I have ever had the privilege of reading, and who has done more than any other to shape how I view and approach the world.

L.E. Modesitt Jr., for making me think about how magic would be integrated into everything about how people lived, and nudging me to consider just where the power for all that magic came from.

D.E. Stevenson, for showing me how much joy one can derive from seeing beloved characters triumph over ordinary problems.

There are so many more that it would be impossible to list them all, but rest assured that many dozens more helped in one way or another.

Second, for the certain specific things that led to the subject matter of this book:

To all the many of us who felt aggrieved that we could not simply enjoy magic school, or wandering Narnia, and to the specific person who bewailed that the greatest crime the Dark Lords commit is to deprive us of the opportunity to explore these worlds.

To everyone involved in the cozy, wonderful adaptations of All Creatures Great and Small, of which this is essentially the answer to "what if we did that, but with wizards?", for helping myself and my family make it through dark days with a comforting light awaiting us.

And finally, to the author of the foreword to the Way of Kings, who so proudly wrote of pushing Mr. Sanderson to ensure that the fabric of existence was at stake in his works. May this work serve as a polite rebuttal to advice I found utterly infuriating.

Third, for all those who nurtured and developed my deep love and interest in history:

Mr. Haydock, I hope that you can feel proud in having turned one of your students who avoided history whenever possible into someone now writing historically-inspired fiction.

To the many wonderful people on r/AskHistorians for the frankly unfathomably mind-boggling work you do, and the many hours of enjoyment and awe you have provided me and my family.

To Dr. Bret C. Devereaux, who provided so much of the understanding needed for the basics of everyday life. May your pedantry on https://acoup.blog/ provide enlightenment to many others.

To Eric Flint, David Drake, and the many other alt-history authors that started me on my journey towards wondering how things could be different.

To Paradox and other game studios for showing me the absolute joy that can be found in righting historical wrongs and making things as we wish they could have been.

To all those in the Empire of Chivalry and Steel, and the rest of the Living History community, for helping me find others living out of our times.

Fourth, for those who helped hone my writing:

To everyone on Tom Vogt's Battlemaster, helping me learn my craft in the trenches. A recommendation for the gentle reader: If you wish to rapidly improve in writing, play a game in which success, friends, lovers, power, and social standing all depend utterly on the quality of your writing.

To the professors, managers, and others who managed to impress upon me the absolute necessity of brevity in writing. As I understand it, it is not common when submitting a draft to an editor for said editor to advise adding more rather than subtracting, and it took many years for me to learn to restrain my natural tendencies toward excess.

To my friends and extended family who patiently read each chapter and helped me understand that yes, in fact, someone besides me could be interested in it.

And finally, for my family:

To my parents who encouraged reading without fail.

To my brother and sister-in-law, who provided incredible and unlooked-for support when I was not sure this would ever be worth the attention of anyone who did not know me personally.

To Grandma, for all the quiet years of joy and wisdom that helped me learn who I wanted to be and to take the steps necessary to become him.

To my wonderful wife and alaurable stepdaughter, for being my best friends and greatest happiness.

No man is an island, so it is said, but more than most I am deeply aware, and deeply grateful, for how much this is a product of standing on the shoulders of giants. I hope my own offering to the great weave of human creativity will at least add a worthy thread to the tapestry.

About the Author

Matthew has been interested in writing since he first read a book about a boy who grew up to be an author (Five Windows, D.E. Stevenson). He's had various twists and turns into science, coding, and business, but writing always lured him back (possibly because that's how he met and caught his wonderful wife). He currently resides with her, his delightful stepdaughter, and two overly-excitable pups in a house cozier than he ever imagined in Reno, Nevada.

MatthewRunyon.com, https://www.campfirewriting.com/user/Dragonlord

www.ingramcontent.com/pod-product-compliance
Lightning Source LLC
Chambersburg PA
CBHW011513100726
47899CB00010BD/3343